IS HEAVEN BIG ENOUGH
For Both of Us?

By G.L. Johnson

authorHOUSE™

1663 LIBERTY DRIVE, SUITE 200
BLOOMINGTON, INDIANA 47403
(800) 839-8640
WWW.AUTHORHOUSE.COM

© 2004 G.L. Johnson
All Rights Reserved.

No part of this book may be reproduced, stored in a retrieval system, or transmitted by any means without the written permission of the author.

First published by AuthorHouse 11/02/04

ISBN: 1-4208-0347-6 (sc)

Printed in the United States of America
Bloomington, Indiana

This book is printed on acid-free paper.

Scripture taken from the King James Version and
Today's New English Version of the Bible.
Permission granted by Rebecca Brown 94-0417
Permission granted by Ed Vogel, Review Journal/Las Vegas Sun 04-0526
Protected under The Victim's Rights Act

*As iron sharpens iron,
so a person sharpens the countenance of their friend.*
Proverbs 27:17 (NKJV)

Table of Contents

Part One Is Heaven Big Enough For Both Of Us? 1

Chapter One Before the beginning . . . darkness. 3
Chapter Two Graduation 7
Chapter Three One Way 11
Chapter Four Las Vegas 15
Chapter Five Family 25
Chapter Six Hollywood........................... 35
Chapter Seven Deliver Us From Evil?........................... 45
Chapter Eight Mountain Man 51
Chapter Nine Summer Breeze 59
Chapter Ten The Curse Is Broken 67
Chapter Eleven Troublemaker 71
Chapter Twelve Is Heaven Big Enough? 83

Part Two Triumph: In Spite Of It All........................... 87

Chapter Thirteen The Question........................... 89
Chapter Fourteen His Kingdom 97
Chapter Fifteen His Purpose 103
Chapter Sixteen The Call 109
Chapter Seventeen Church........................... 115
Chapter Eighteen Our Healer........................... 121
Chapter Nineteen The Answer 127
Chapter Twenty Your Hope Of Glory 133

Part One

Is Heaven Big Enough For Both Of Us?

Chapter One
Before the beginning . . . darkness.

Las Vegas, Nevada – 1964

Sentenced to 20 years in prison for the horribly brutal rape and attempted murder of a local women near Sunrise Mountain, Patrick C. McKenna, aka Charles Allen James, barely 18 at the time of the attack, showed no emotion, as the jury read the verdict.

Patrick beat the woman without mercy before sodomizing her. A stick, which had a protruding nail, had been his weapon.

But this was not his first attack, and this was not the beginning.

It began on August 8, 1946 in Leadville, Colorado, when Patrick took his first breath, entering into this world, crying.

Could his mother's arms be enough to guard him from the pain of being the firstborn in this, his family. Only his mother knew of the punches that she had endured from her husband following his nightly use of whiskey. He was a mean drunk, but she hid it well.

Smiling at her sweet little baby, she hoped that, together, they would be able to handle the pain that her husband could cause them.

With each pregnancy, she is able to hide her abuse, and soon the house is filled with boys, five in all.

What a happy family they appear to be, but the authorities know the truth behind their smiles, yet they do nothing to help.

Soon, Patrick's family move to Nevada, and try to start over, hoping that the abuse would end. But moving does not solve their problems, and starting over does not ease their pain.

So far, Patrick's life has been full of pain and suffering at the hands of an alcoholic father. Beatings are common for both him and his mother, but he is strong and able to block out the pain as he would stand in for his brothers and take the abuse for them. But, seeing his mother beaten, bothers him deeply, and a profound hatred for his father is developing.

Wanting so much to defend her, he plans an attempt to stop the abuse, standing outside the door holding tightly to a baseball bat.

G.L. Johnson

The cries of his mother as she is beaten, call out to him, but he is unable to muster up the nerve, and that makes him angry, not only at his father, but at himself for being a coward.

But he is not a coward, he is a little boy, and a little boy should not have to defend his mother from his drunken father.

But this was a time when the authorities turned a blind eye on domestic violence, and society blamed the child rather than the parent.

Patrick was a victim, a child, with no one to protect him.

But he had great inner strength, and so he stood still and let his father beat him for flunking out of a couple of classes at school.

Then, rather than go with bruises, he decides to skip school just for a little while. At least until the bruises fade away.

But his mother somehow doesn't understand that he is embarrassed by his father's abuse, so hoping that the system will be able to "reform" him, she sends him to Spring Mountain Youth Camp, for truancy.

But reformation would not be offered to Patrick.

Instead, there would be humiliation, molestation, and abuse by the very ones assigned to protect him. Again the victim, a 13 year old boy, with no help in sight, is chained to the flagpole naked, beaten, and left overnight to be used as an example to the others.

This disciplinary tactic was confirmed, by camp administrator, Richard Ries, and the guards have since been referred to as,

"Perverted, degenerate, psychotic, sadistic guards who beat and brutalize the kids and turn them into monsters."

His reformers had turned his pain into intense hatred and by the time he is released, he is a monster, ready to cause others pain.

In 1960, before his 14th birthday, Patrick is arrested for stabbing a man and sent to juvenile jail in Elko, where his abuse would surely continue.

He hardens his heart toward the authorities, as he grows to become a young man in need of a connection, in need of real reformation, in need of so much more.

But it could not come from his abusers, and it could not come from inside of a cell. It could only come from inside of his heart.

Soon after his release he finds her.

Yes, finally, he meets and falls in love with a girl, and her love seems to mellow him, as they await the birth of their daughter.

Patrick is still so young, only 17, so there is hope for him. Maybe he will find peace in his new family.

Is Heaven Big Enough for Both of Us?

Becoming a father will change things for Patrick, as he is determined to do right by his girls. He squares his shoulders with pride in his new God given responsibility. Love is making him a new man. Reformation is coming from within.

But on that special day, his little girl is born, lifeless, and with her death, Patrick loses the last of his hope in God, and he is now determined to prove that God does not exist. How could God possible exist?

"If God is real, than I will make him pay." He vows.

So now, with hatred and anger, hand in hand, fueling his rage, he beats the woman over and over with the stick. Her blood quenches his thirst as he proves to her that God is not real.

As his violent rampage continues, in his hatred, Patrick brutally beats and nearly kills a young man. His name, Bob Coffin.

Guilty of rape and attempted murder, he is now on his way to prison. Could he survive 20 years? Could the abuse reform him?

He needed to escape and soon, so he wastes no time and within one year, the prison guards find the bars to his cell cut in his first attempt to escape, and by the next year he is successful by hiding inside of garbage cans. He is easily thrown out with the trash.

Free, yet for some reason, he gives up and surrenders only to escape again two years later at age 22, this time, taking a guard hostage, he helps several of the inmates to escape with him, which earns him a good reputation on the inside. They are captured, and put back behind bars.

"Kill the pig. Kill the pig." The inmates chant, as Patrick escapes again, this time holding a knife to a guard's belly.

He is not free for long, and once more behind bars, but he doesn't waste any time as he immediately plans his next escape.

Escaping has become a game to him, something to keep his mind occupied. Before long he is ready to make his next attempt but just 2 ½ months before his 30th birthday, he is granted parole. Paroled? Only 12 years out of 20 served. Let out, 8 years early. June 1, 1976

Patrick is given another chance at life, and he is relatively young enough to still have some hope at a future. He had so hoped to be free for his 30th birthday, and somehow, now, he was.

So, he looks for a job and 5 days later is contracted to kill a man. But he changes his mind, botching the job, deciding to let the man go, if he promises to leave the area, and instead of killing him, Patrick kidnaps the man's girlfriend, and brutally sodomizes her, beating her nearly to death.

G.L. Johnson

Parole is revoked. June 6, 1976. Patrick would be spending his 30th birthday in prison after all.

But just 1 year and 9 months later, the prison system is satisfied with his performance, and now, having only served 14 years out of his 20 year sentence, he is released. Perhaps it was his good behavior?

March 19, 1978, Patrick Charles McKenna is again a free man. Now, 31 ½ years old, he has spent most of his youth and all, but a handful of days, out of his adulthood, behind bars, being taught how to be a monster, from the inside out.

Patrick has learned how to survive in the jungle of hatred and pain, instead of the love and nurturing that he had so hoped for in his youth. His youth? It had ended before it had ever even begun.

And now they have released him, making him free, to do what ever he wants . . . what ever he feels like doing.

Three days later, my story begins.

Chapter Two
Graduation

"Big mouth, know it all, fat, pain in the . . . Why did I have you? I can't wait till you turn 18." My mother's voice haunted me.

"You're not even mine. I was golfing when your mother got knocked up." My father's voice chimed in.

It seemed like there was nothing but fighting, pain, anger, and filth, terrible filth. But, that was the best that they could do.

I don't know why I always expected more, but I did. So I was not surprised when I found out that Mom was leaving Dad for the Sunday school teacher at our "family" church. Not surprised, but very angry. I knew that they were all sinners going to Hell and I told them all about it.

I wasn't very popular at home, and when our new "Dad" moved in, I rebelled. Giving him a taste of hell on earth, I was all the terrible things that they called me! But there was another part of me that only I knew of, deep inside.

So while my mother was hooking up with a man, I was hooking up with The Main Man, Jesus. I loved Him with all of my heart, and I just knew that He loved me. If only I knew how to act. I didn't have a clue.

I did stay involved at school and I got good grades. I was the president of the Pep Club, and it was my job to motivate others to get involved. My heart was in it, so I excelled.

But this morning, yes this morning! I wonder what today will bring. I'm 18. I am an adult. The rules change today. I get to be my own boss.

"Well, Boss, better get up and start your special day." I told myself.

March 22, 1978. In just two months I'll graduate. Then I can get a job and an apartment, and run my life right. Maybe even clean up the filth.

Yes. Good morning, Gina! HAPPY Birthday to me!

Life looked hopeful as I headed down the stairs.

"Hey, what are you doing home?" I said, surprised to see my sister, Vicky sitting at the table.

"Spring break." She answered smugly. She's been away at college and it's been so nice. But, since she'll only be home a couple days and today is my day . . . we won't fight.

But as I stood there, I felt that same ugly feeling that, as I put it, comes out of the walls at our house.

"I think I'll just go for a bike ride." I said to myself, grabbing my bike. But before I could get to the door, Mom stopped me.

"Where do you think you are going?" She snapped at me.

"Hey Mom, just out." I answered.

I sensed trouble as I headed for the door, pushing my bike a little faster. My sister, Anna sat quietly by watching.

"As long as you live in my house . . ." Mom started, again.

"Mom, I'm 18 years old . . ." I began.

"You will come and go when I say that you can come and go." She pulled my bike. I pulled back. Then, she slapped me, and without thinking, I slapped her back.

"Mom, I'm sorry. I . . ."

BOOM.

"You get out of here and don't you ever come back." Vicky screamed as she waved her weapon. The broom.

I ran outside before I was forced to hurt her. There I stood.

"Happy Birthday," I thought, "Now, where am I going to go?" Just then the front door opened and out came a huge box with all my clothes and personal belongings. "And what am I going to do with all of that?"

Now being immobile, with all this stuff, I decided to go to the neighbor's house and ask if I could wait there for Mom to chill out, and Vicky to go back to college, so that I could go home.

As I continued to wait, the hours turned to days, and the neighbor's smile turned to concern as my baby sister Lisa visited.

"Mom's really mad, and Dad says there's no way you can come back. Oh, Gina, what are you going to do?" She cried at the thought of me being gone, and she worried that I might try suicide.

"No way!" I assured her. I knew that I was special to Jesus and I knew that He loved me and would protect me. "I will serve the Lord." I said. If only I knew how. "Where are you God. I know that you are real, I can feel you. And where are my teachers?" I asked.

I had seen so much sin within the church that my heart was hardened to both sin and church. Not only had our church helped my mother to leave her husband, and her children's father, they threw my dad out when he found out about the "affair". He asked the pastor for help, and they told him to leave and to not come back.

Yes, it was a little twisted but then again look at what was going on behind closed office doors. The pastor, himself, was gay and dating the youth director, all which seemed to go unnoticed by the youth's parents.

The last place that I would be looking for God would be in "Church."

My dad! That's it. I'll find my dad. But the last time I spoke to him I was eleven. Seven years have passed. He could be almost anywhere. Although he did talk a lot about Las Vegas . . .

"Hello, Information?" I took a deep breath. "Do you have a listing for a . . . you do?" I dialed the phone. "Hello, Dad . . ."

There goes GRADUATION . . .

Chapter Three
One Way

No return flight. Well, that was just fine with me. It would be a cold day in July before I would ever be going back there!

Besides, I've always liked my dad. I don't remember a lot about him, but I do know that I like him. I sure do hope that he likes me. I'm sure that he does. After all, wasn't it me who took his side through the divorce, and I even still treat mom bad because of what she did to him, and it was me who found him. I really do hope that he likes me.

"Would you like something to drink?" The stewardess smiled. I nodded as she tried to reassure me. "Try not to be nervous, we will be landing soon."

"Thanks, I'll be fine." I smiled back.

I'm nervous, but not about landing. I can hardly believe that just a few days ago, I was . . . seventeen.

"Oh Jesus, let him be a good dad, who will teach me the right ways, and let him be a good example and oh please let him love me. Please let him love me."

I guess that anything would be better than the example that I got from my mom. Once, she had given me the sound advice that with my female parts, I would never have to go hungry.

What could she have possibly been thinking, telling me that?

Mom was an entertainer, a tap dancer. She took her show on the road, performing in so called night clubs all over down south; New Orleans, Florida, Mississippi. She was "Miss Personality on Taps." I still remember the little bitty costumes. They didn't cover much, but they sparkled. These were the days of Burlesque.

And Dad, he was the MC. He started the show with his humor. He was funny. But the joke was on him. They got married and started having babies. But still, the show must go on.

There she was, so beautiful.

I watched in silence as she danced, wearing a sparkling red sequence costume, holding a large gray feather fan in front of her as she tapped danced across the stage. The beat was slow yet filled with excitement.

Her naked leg peaked out from behind the fan, as she allowed a quick look at her shiny costume, teasing the audience.

They cheer, as she spins to the beat of the drums, holding the fan high above her head, and as the spin ends she is once more hidden behind her fan. The fan has become a piece of the artwork that she has created.

I notice a pain in her eyes as she reaches out with her feathers, and then, disappearing once more behind them, she taps and spins. She is lost in her dance as the passion of the music drives her on.

There are more cheers as she raises her fan far above her head, as the music comes to an end. She leans her head far back, as she makes her final pose, her breasts reaching toward heaven. The stage lights go black as a single red spotlight shines down on her bare skin, and like a statue, she remains motionless, as the light slowly fades away.

I just stood there breathless, amazed at her breasts.

Out of no where, Vicky grabs me by the hand, pulling me away from the stage. She is yelling at me.

"Get out of here, Gina. You are going to get us all in trouble."

Mom runs off of the stage and suddenly she has gone from glamorous to horror movie in seconds. She begins speaking bitterly to my dad.

"That's it. That is the last show I'm doing. No more counting on a baby sitter. I'm going back to Ohio and settling down, with or without you. I quit." She complains as she puts on her clothes.

She then storms out of the stage door and down the alley toward the trailer park. Dad is following behind her with Anna and Vicky along side. Vicky has my hand, pulling me.

"Okay, okay. Listen, I can't quit in the middle of the tour, so you go to Ohio and get a place and I'll finish out our tour with the rest of the girls. Then I'll quit next season. Betty we have a contract. We can't just quit." He protests.

"I know you can't quit. You're too busy, while I'm dancing to watch your own kids." She accuses him, for she was not a fool. "But, you're right, we do have a contract, and I'm not giving up the money. You can get Bambi to do my spot, since she's already doing you, and Sindy can move to Bambi's spot. You can give them my costumes. I just can't do this anymore. The children need a place to call home. You can come see us between tours. You don't have to quit. I'll be fine alone."

She said, assuring him that she would be okay, and then she turned around to look at him, with a look of disgust, adding,

"Besides, I think I'm pregnant." She turns and goes inside, leaving my dad standing there with his three daughters.

"Maybe we will get a brother?" He suggested.

The airplane continued on toward Las Vegas as I continued on to my next memory. Our first home.

We ran around the house, playing carelessly, as mom went on with her life, partying inside, with the boy from across the street.

She was right. She would be just fine without my dad. So, she went on with her affair, while he went on with his. Only, it was different now that he was the one who was being cheated on.

When we saw dad drive up, we new that mom was in for some trouble. We needed to act quick, so, Vicky ran to worn mom and we gathered around the car, to stall dad.

"Dad, Dad, you're home." I cheered, hugging him before he even got out of the car. I sat on his lap in the front seat, wrapping my arms around his neck. "I missed you daddy." I added.

I didn't let him out of the car until mom came out of the house. Her hair was a mess and she had buttoned her shirt up wrong. She had picked up Lisa and was holding her on her hip, but she quickly put her down as he approached her. She looked nervous.

"Hi baby, you're home." She said with a sexy whisper, meeting him on the top step. She wrapped herself around him, kissing him, passionately. She was sexy, but he was suspicious.

He stood back, looking her over, as she continued.

"How long do we have?" She said, smiling.

He wants her, but he passes her without speaking, disappearing into the house. She follows him, looking back at her children.

Hours pass and it is dark when the door finally opens. I get up from the porch step and go inside. It is dark inside, and too quiet.

A light shines from the TV in my mother's room. Dad is sitting at the dining room table in the dark, and I feel the tension as I tiptoe past him. I stop and hold my breath, motionless, after tripping over a whiskey bottle, hoping for the quiet to return.

"Gina, come here." Dad grunts. I walk cautiously toward him.

"I'm only going to ask you this one time. If you don't tell me the truth and I find out that you're a liar, and I'll cut out your tongue."

He grabs me by my arms, looking deep into my eyes.

"Now tell me, is that boy across the street coming over to visit your mother when I'm not home?" He snarled, glaring into my eyes.

G.L. Johnson

"No dad. I have never seen him come over here. I swear, never."

He pushed me away and as I ran out of the room, past my mother's open bedroom door, I could not resist looking in.

I peek into her room. It was filthy. Clothes thrown on the floor, and trash everywhere. There is an empty whiskey bottle and glasses on the night-stand, where a cigarette burns low in the ashtray. Lights flicker from the TV, where the sounds of a woman groaning, as if in terrible pain, are coming out. I stopped to look. What was that they were doing?

I turned to see my mother, sprawled across the bed, face down, naked. I moved toward her, pulling her hair back from her face.

There was blood around her mouth and nose, where he had beaten her. She was passed out. Crying, I wipe the blood from her face with her sheet and then, I covered her up.

"Oh mom, if he knew, he'd kill you. Why mom? Why can't that boy just stay away from you." I whispered, kissing her on her cheek, and tucking her in. "Goodnight, Mom."

I went to bed, and later that night, Anna woke me up, suddenly.

"Quick, Gina, get up, call the police." She whispered. "Dad's going to kill Mom." She warned.

Well, not if I could help it. I ran down to the bottom of the stairs where Dad was waving a pistol at my mom's head.

"Don't." I jumped in front of her, challenging my father as he pressed the gun to her head. Suddenly, all four of us girls were protecting her from Dad.

He was drunk. He stunk so bad when he drank. I'll never forget that awful smell. I swore, right then, that I was not going to be like either of them. No way.

"The fasten seat belt light has come on, we will be landing in a moment. Please fasten your seat belts." The stewardess said.

We're here.

What am I doing here?

Here I go . . .

Chapter Four
Las Vegas

"My god, you're fat. What has your mother done to you?"

A simple "Hello" would have been much more appropriate. And probably hurt a lot less.

"I know Dad." I agreed.

He was right. It was all my mom's fault. He had nothing to do with my insecurity and low self esteem or my lack of self worth. It was all because of "her".

As he passed me a joint, he gave me his first bit of good advice.

"The first thing we have to do is get you on the pill." He suggested. "You know sex is expected in this town. No one gets anything for free."

"What a pig." I thought as I handed him the joint.

Little did I know that he too would be expecting his way, after all, I was "his" and I did belong to him.

"This is your room." He said, before excusing himself to go and make us a drink. "What do you like?" He asked.

"I like white wine." I told him, and off he went.

I started to unpack, but then decided to take a bath. I put on my robe and left my room. He was sitting on the couch.

"Can I take a bath?" I asked him as I headed for the bathroom.

"Oh, can't we just talk for a minuet? It's been so long. I want to show you these pictures of you when you were a baby. Here, I poured you some wine." He offered me the glass. I took it.

"Come here, sit. Look at you." He put the pictures in my hand as I sat next to him on the couch. The wine was wonderful and I was really thirsty, so I drank it down quickly. Before rushing to get me another glass, he lit a joint and handed it to me.

"I'll be right back." He said.

I took a long hit off the joint and held it in.

"That robe looks hot. This isn't Ohio anymore." He said, returning.

He was right. It wasn't Ohio. I was feeling quite hot.

He sat close, leaning toward me, to give me a "shot gun" with the joint. I took in all of the smoke trying to prove to him that I could handle it. He was impressed.

"Give me one?" He asked with excitement.

"Here." I said, blowing the smoke into his mouth.

"Here." He said, handing me my drink.

Not even noticing that the drugs had not yet dissolved, I drank them down with my white wine.

"Come here, I want to show you my girlfriend." He jumped up and grabbed my drink, motioning me to follow. Innocently, I did.

"She's on this tape. Up next." He was pointing to the TV, but suddenly I felt as though I would fall, so I reached out for the bed.

"Oh, I'm dizzy." I said.

"Sit here. I don't think that I could pick you up." He laughed. "Here, push back. Lay here till you feel better. It's really hot in here, maybe you should take off that hot robe." He reached over to turn on the fan, and with it, a red spotlight came on over the bed.

"Mellow" I joked. "You're right, it is really hot in here."

He helped me to loosen my robe, but I held it close to my chest as I lay back into his pillows.

"You know, Gina, I hated your mother for taking you away from me. I missed you so much." He told me.

"Oh dad, I missed you, too." I assured him.

He sat by my head, caressing my hair. I felt safe. Drunk, but safe. I tried to sit up, but I couldn't.

"I can't move. Do you think that it's the wine?" I asked him.

"It's probably just the move to the desert. You're not used to the dry weather." He made up excuses, trying to get my robe off. "It's the heat. Here, take off that robe." He insisted. "Are you sure that you can't move?" He questioned me.

"Yes, I'm sure, I can't move." I answered, unable to stop him from pulling open my robe. I watched his eyes widened with delight as he pulled it open.

"You've grown." He smiled. "You do know that you belong to me, don't you?" He asked, as he reached down, searching for the answer, gasping as he realized my innocence.

"Yes, my little girl, you do belong to me." He whispered, as he reached into the drawer of the night stand. "You are all mine, my little girl, all mine." He said, slobbering over me.

He turned on the switch and I heard a hum as my body jumped. What was he doing to me?

"Ahhhhh" I gasped, screaming in horror, my body trembled.

I closed my eyes, waiting for him to finish. Crying on the inside, I wondered how he had gotten so twisted to do this to me.

I knew that I had to get out of there, and fast. I would just have to survive on my own, but I couldn't stay.

Now I knew why my mother wanted him out of our lives, him and his sick ideas of owning his children.

"God, please make it go fast. Please." I begged.

I knew just what to do and how to do it.

"First, I need to hustle up a man with cash and sell my body for a meal ticket. My folks sure have prepared me well."

Respect? Who? Me? My trick? My parents? My Pastor? There was someone. Joseph. He was known as the king of dreams in the bible. I had only heard of him in Sunday school. Joseph's brothers had dumped all over him and had even sold him into slavery, but he always ended up on top, he was always victorious. As a slave, a prisoner, and a leader, he stayed hooked up to God.

That was my only hope, to stay hooked up to God. But I was able to block out my conscience and my feelings, and listen to my mind, which was programmed for destruction.

Three and a half months passed . . .

I got my diploma! I also got filled to the brim with demons. I hate my life but mostly I hate men. They are such pigs. I only turn a trick when rent is due or if I'm hungry. $100 goes along way in Vegas, since I'm not old enough to gamble.

My insides are torn constantly. No matter what mom said, I know this is wrong. I just know that this is wrong.

"God, I know this is wrong, and I promise to change, I just need help." I made the decision to quit selling myself. I was through with it all. I told my friend, Cherry, of my plan to clean up my life.

She wanted to do the same, so we decided to help each other and quit together. We celebrated with a night out at our favorite disco.

"I'm telling you, if I have to let another man touch me, I think that I might kill him." I confessed to Cherry. She understood.

Heading home we giggled about our plans to get real jobs and start over. We had high hopes mixed with hope of getting high.

"Do you want to smoke a joint?" Cherry asked.

"Roll it up." I said, stepping into her room, ever ready to party.

POW. I got sucker punched right in the nose, and as I slid down the front door, momentarily stunned, I realized that there was a man locking the door. As he turned around, and I saw his eyes, I knew that we were in for big trouble.

I was bleeding pretty heavy from my nose, and I felt numb. It could have been the punch, could have been the booze. I didn't care why, but I was glad to be numb.

Then, he showed us his shotgun and his knife and told us all about the women that he had met up with already. He shared details and how they pleaded for their lives, bragging of how he had placed their limbs around the desert.

I studied his face, as I listened to his anger, while he boasted.

At first I wasn't sure if he was telling the truth or just trying to be some tuff guy, trying to impress us with his violent history.

But then as I watched his eyes, I realized that this was genuine hatred. Someone had hit a nerve, a deep down nerve.

I didn't know what to think, and I didn't realize how scared I should have been. As time passed, I began to realize.

He then made us take off our clothes and he tied us up, putting nooses around our necks, so that if we did get too far apart, or pulled, it would tighten around our necks, making us choke.

He told us of how he had shot a man in the back of his head, and his eyes glowed as he remembered beating another woman bloody with a stick, and then licking her blood as he sodomized her, bragging that he made her taste death.

"The first time for me, I was 13. They tied me to the pole when they were finished. The f——ing pigs." He grunted, pushing his body toward my face, trying to force himself into my mouth.

Refusing him service triggered a series of punches to my head, until I opened my mouth for him, but still I refused, so he pushed me away and then kicked me in the face. I saw stars, but I didn't pass out. I tasted my own blood, as it flowed from my nose.

He then, very graphically told us how he was going to cut us up. Starting with our faces . . .he held the knife to Cherry's face as he pushed himself toward her. She was much too afraid to refuse, quickly opening her mouth. He howled with pleasure, banging her head against the wall with each thrust. Trying to satisfy his groans, she knew that her life depended on his pleasure, and she refused to disappoint him. He pushed hard, seeking to end her ability to breathe, as he blocked her airway.

"Taste death." He yelled, as she struggled for air. Her arms waving frantically as he gave no intentions of stopping. She was dying and I was next. In the middle of all this torture, I said to myself in a whisper.

"Oh my God, I sure could go for that joint."

Suddenly, Patrick stopped and jumped up.

"I'll be right back." He said. "Don't talk." And then he split.

"What are we going to do?" Cherry cried, as she gasped for air. She was trembling and she looked terrible.

Then, I remembered. Cherry was talking to this psycho at the pool the other day. That's right. Oh my God, she let him in.

"Cherry, do you know him?" I started to accuse her.

"I thought he was pretty cool. I didn't even charge him. Oh my God, what have I done? He's gonna kill us, Gina, I just know it." She cried as she rambled on about wanting to live.

"Don't be afraid." I felt bad for her. She was terrified.

"All I know is that I sure could go for that joint right about now." I said, trying to break the tension.

Thinking that wanting a joint was what got me into this mess, I laughed at myself. Perfect timing. In walked Patrick.

He looked surprised to see me smiling. He could sense that I wasn't afraid of him. Yet, in obedience, I just sat there, waiting.

"Huh." He grunted as he pulled a plastic bag out of his pants.

"Yes, Pot! God is good," I thought to myself.

He then forced us to smoke a huge joint about half way before making us eat the rest, and as I finished the silent praise for the pot, Patrick got up and began beating Cherry in the face, again.

Over and over he punched her as the blood flew everywhere.

He looked at me a couple times but decided to keep hitting her. I finally asked him to stop.

"Okay, then let's see what you've got." He hit me a couple times, but then, he stopped and went back to hitting Cherry.

Ready for more sex, he grabbed the knife in one hand and Cherry's hair with the other, forcing her face-down onto the bed. He forced himself into her as he pushed her face into the pillow. I watched in horror as his eyes glowed as he raped her.

Then he looked over at me and our eyes locked. We both froze for a moment and then he jumped up grabbing his shotgun from under the bed. And as he took a moment to load it, I began to fear.

Up to this point, Cherry had been getting the worst of it, and there was nothing that I could do but watch and wait for some sort of an ending to all this torture, but I didn't like the way he was looking at me now.

Cherry was still on the bed, face-down, lying motionless.

"Turn over, Bitch." He yelled at Cherry. She obeyed his command but when she saw his shotgun she began to sob.

"I'm gonna shoot my gun inside of you." He threatened her as he pushed it hard against her thighs forcing them apart. Standing at the foot of the bed, he pushed it inside and then jerked it hard.

"Bang." He yelled, as if he had fired it.

I jumped and Cherry screamed in horror. Patrick threw his head back, laughing. He grabbed her, flipping her over on her face, he climb on top of her, sitting on her back. He pushed her face hard into the pillow, grunting his demands at her.

"Taste death. Taste it." He yelled, as he smothered her.

When he finished, he kicked her to the floor and laid in the middle of the bed across the top of the sheet that was around our necks.

Cherry looked dead, but I could see that she was still breathing. She just laid there, not moving. I looked at Patrick, and waited.

As he lay there smoking a cigarette, he began his story,

"This is all my f——ing mother's fault. Once . . ." He began. His eyes were full of hatred. I felt so bad for him.

"They tried to make me a fag. But I'm not a f——ing fag am I? Am I?" He nudged Cherry, with his foot, seeking confirmation.

She looked up at him in terror, shaking her head, no, as she pulled herself up off of the floor.

"No. You're not a fag?" she assured him. "You're swell."

"Shut up, Bitch." He said kicking her back down onto the floor.

It was easy to understanding how he could hate so much, after hearing the stories that he told. He continued his confession, session, assuring us that there was plenty of sex available in prison.

"A simple blow job can save your life." He admitted, smiling down at Cherry, but then he glared at me.

"One time, we put firecrackers up inside this bitch. I wish I had one for you now." He laughed, kicking at Cherry with his foot.

As he bragged, I realized that he had been through way too much abuse for one person. Enough to cause intense hatred. I believe that he was most angry with his mother. He blamed her.

It seemed like we had been there forever, when I noticed that Patrick had fallen asleep.

"Too much excitement." I said to myself, watching him sleep.

"Who could he hate enough to kill people? It had to be his mother. Who else? Maybe his father? Possibly himself?" I felt really bad for him, as I just sat there, watching and waiting.

Cherry had fallen back asleep, too. She was a bloody mess.

Looking down at myself, I saw that I was covered in my own blood, and naked. I thought of what I must have looked like, 250 pounds, tied up, naked. I shook my head, in disbelief.

"Yuck" I laughed to myself, adding, "I've even bored him to death."

Patrick woke up and once again caught me smiling. He looked at me a little puzzled. Something had to be wrong with me to not be scared or mad. I was just kind of waiting. I wondered if any of his other victims had smiled at him before he killed them.

"Hey, how ya doing? Are you okay?" He asked, as he untied me.

I nodded as I rubbed my wrists and ankles, watching him.

"How are you?" I asked him, quietly.

"I'm okay." He said as he dialed the phone. "Mom, it's me." He said into the phone. "No, I stayed with a friend. No. Yes, I'm being good, mother. Yes. Yes. Yes."

"Please don't make him mad lady." I thought.

I could see he was getting very irritated by her. With his calmness changing to annoyance, he slammed down the phone and started pacing. He was suddenly that other person again.

"I am so bored with you. I'll just go ahead and kill you now."

Cherry's eyes filled with terror as he grabbed her hair forcing her head back and her neck out. I saw blood as the knife began its mission. Now was the time for prayer.

With all of my heart, I prayed a silent prayer.

"Oh God, I am not asking to live, I know that I am dead . . ." I took a deep breath . . .

"But, please, if you can forgive me of my sins, so that I can come to heaven. I just want to see Jesus. I just want to see Jesus."

As I finished the last prayer that I thought that I would ever pray, I looked up. There stood Jesus, in the middle of the light.

"Jesus!" Was all that I could say. The room was filled with gentleness and great peace.

"I am here with you, always. Don't be afraid." Jesus assured, "I need you to tell people that I am real and that I am alive. I need you to tell Patrick that I am real, too, and that I love him" He said.

"I will." I replied, "I will." And then, I looked over at Patrick.

He had stopped cutting Cherry's neck and was staring at me. It was as if time was standing still, as we looked at each other. I wondered if he had seen Jesus, but I didn't get the chance to ask.

"I can't kill you," He told Cherry, "because I can't kill Gina."

He dropped her and grabbed his shotgun, wrapping his jacket around it. He then headed for the door, but suddenly stopped and grabbed me by my hair forcing my bloody face toward his.

"If you tell anyone, I'll come back and kill you. Do you understand. Don't tell anyone. Promise me, now." He said.

Pulling my hair hard inside his fist, he glared into my eyes.

"I promise." I whispered. "I promise."

He let go of me and walked out. The door shut behind him.

Cherry started sobbing as I removed the noose from around her neck. Untying her, I praised Jesus, for sparing my life.

I knew beyond a shadow of a doubt that Jesus was real. I would never be the same again. I saw Jesus. In the middle of the trouble that I definitely did deserve, Jesus heard me. He took the time to come into my sin filled life, Himself, saving me from destruction.

Cherry took off, and I knew that I would not see her again.

But I couldn't just leave town and let Patrick continue to hurt others. I just couldn't. I had to do something before it happened again, so I went to the police and filed my report.

I broke my promise to Patrick and I told. But, they had to get him off the streets before he was able to hurt any one else, and the next day they found him outside of Cherry's apartment, lurking around and talking about needing to finish a "job". He came back.

He was arrested, and without bail, he sits behind bars, awaiting his court date. Hopefully, we will now be safe from his abuse.

That night, from a hotel room in Las Vegas, I called my mother.

"Mom, can I come home?" I couldn't believe that I needed her.

"Yes." She said. "Of course you can come home."

The bus ride will take a week, so I'll have plenty of time to plan my next move. But, I do know a few things for sure.

1. Jesus is real, He's alive, and He loves me.

2. He said that He would never leave me. No matter what kind of trouble that I get myself into, He'll be there to get me out.
3. I know that I have a purpose. Why would Jesus come Himself to save me without a purpose? I have a purpose.

As I arrived in Ohio, I thought, this must be a cold day, in July.

Chapter Five
Family

"Why didn't you tell me you were leaving?" Tina asked me.

Tina was everything I could have hoped for in a friend. She didn't care about any of the mistakes I had made. All she cared about was keeping our friendship alive.

"Don't do it again." She said as we made plans that if I ever went west again, she'd ride with me to "keep me out of trouble!"

Tina was the most beautiful girl I knew. She was smart, too. Her family was everything I had wanted mine to be. Through them, I learned how people were supposed to be. So different from my family. She had brothers who loved and protected her, sisters who admired and looked up to her, and parents who respected her. Her dad was really strict. But they taught her right from wrong.

Tina was my mentor. She taught me all the things my parents should have. She was the most important part of my sanity when I came home. I'll never forget her words of wisdom after I told her what had happened to me in Las Vegas.

"All the answers are in the bible." She said. "Everything you need to know is in the bible."

I got myself a bible, but it looked so big.

"Where should I start." I said to myself.

"Where do you start anytime you read a book?"

His soft sweet voice lifted me up. I responded.

"Jesus! You're here. Of course. You said you would be. I'll start at the beginning. I will read my bible from cover to cover and then, I will start over and read it again. I want to know it all!"

I never knew that there would be so much to learn.

"Jesus, give me the answers. Whenever I speak let the words come from you. When people look at me, let them see you. Help me to serve you, in the middle of it all." I prayed.

"Jesus freak, that's what they call people like you. You better stop talking about God." Mom advised. "There has got to be something in your life that is more important than God or something is wrong with you." She barked her disapproval.

I should have guessed her response. She didn't believe that I had seen Jesus and she was ashamed that I had been raped. I wasn't to tell anyone in the family.

I really didn't understand how being raped was any worse than any of the sex that I had the pleasure of experiencing.
1. When a man pays a desperate girl for sex, he is raping her.
2. When a "Daddy" tells his little girl that she belongs to him, he is raping her.
3. When drugs, guns or knives are used, it is rape.

There are many forms of rape and it is all abuse, but if you have been raped, don't be ashamed. It's not you that should feel shame, but the one that hurt you.

Well, I couldn't stay with my mom long. I needed a plan. The phone rang, just in time. It was my dad, the lessor of two evils.

Grandma was sick and needed a live-in helper. If I was interested, I could come and take care of her. Perfect timing.

"California, here I come." I sang, packing my car.

It just so happened that Patrick's court date was coming up, so I could stop in Nevada and testify on my way to California.

Tina took a vacation and we planned our trip. She drove with me to Las Vegas, stayed a couple of days, and then she went home.

I went to Carson City to testify. January 5, 1979.

When I arrived at court, I found out that I was the only witness that had shown up, and that without my testimony, Patrick would walk. I was the only witness, and I had promised him that I would not tell.

But, I couldn't let him hurt anyone else, so I pointed him out to the jury. I successfully stopped him from hurting anyone else, so I thought. I took a deep breath, as they read the verdict.

"Guilty." The judge announced, ready for sentencing.

Patrick was sentenced to three life terms plus 75 years in prison, and was sent back to his jail cell, where his new cell mate, 20 year old, J.J. Nobles, quietly waited. A young boy in the wrong place at the wrong time.

J.J. was new to the Las Vegas jail system. He had been there for about two weeks on a non-violent, burglary charge.

That night, still irritated by the jury's decision, Patrick challenged J.J. to a game of chess as they drank bootleg alcohol.

After winning the chess game, and feeling powerful, Patrick demands sex as payment, and J.J. refuses him service, which angers a

Is Heaven Big Enough for Both of Us?

drunken Patrick, who without mercy, grabs J.J. by the neck. Patrick's eyes glow as he takes J.J.'s life with his bare hands.

The victim had become a habitual victimizer and a cold blooded killer. The evidence proves his guilt without a doubt, and Patrick is convicted of murder. There would be no mercy in his future.

Had I cost J.J. his life by putting Patrick behind bars? I can't bare to think about it now, so I'll think about it tomorrow.

Today, I needed to think about getting out of town. I didn't feel safe in Nevada, so I moved on to California, to meet my grandma.

Grandma, Lucia. She was something. But it was my aunt that I was most taken by. Aunt Ronda. I felt bad for her, but then, when I met my cousin, Mandie, my heart broke for her.

Lucia stepped off of the boat from Sicily in New York City in 1920.

She married my grandpa just days later, at age 14, because that was the arrangement that her father had agreed to. She would have done almost anything to come to America. But, she had no idea what she was going to have to do. Her new husband was a pervert. He liked things that horrified her, things that involved his children.

But who would have known, and who could she tell? She would simply have to perform or suffer the consequences.

"You belong to me." He told my father as he tucked him into bed that night, passing the curse on to his son.

Well, let me tell you, it stops here. I will not let it happen to my children. That is if I ever have children. I sure as heck don't want a husband, let alone a child. No thank you.

With their perverted sex, came five children and much more responsibility than Grandpa wanted. So, out the door he went, leaving Lucia all alone with a family to feed.

Grandma had to work, which forced her to leave her children unattended for most of the time. Aunt Judy was the oldest, so at 12 she was in charge. Her dad would visit her when ever he wanted company.

Child Services did not think that Judy was old enough to sit with 10, 9, 8, and 5 year-old siblings, and they felt that supervision was more important than food. I think that they were right.

Lucia lost her children to the system, although she eventually got Ronda and Billy, the two youngest, and Judy, the oldest back.

My dad and his brother James were put in the Children's Home until they ran away, hooking up with the Mob, who helped them to stay "free." Dad had no desire to go home, or to his father.

G.L. Johnson

He made enough money running little errands and doing little jobs that he could live nicely at the sweet age of 10. Remember, hotel rooms were less than $1 a day, and movies were 10 cents.

Dad was street-smart, and he found out young that he didn't need to sell his body for money, although it would have been good money at his sweet young age. He found that he could do just fine selling his girlfriends, and they would do anything for him.

"He was a real ladies man, by 13. King Kong, Jr." Aunt Ronda laughed. "he had at least 5 girls working for him."

She continued to tell of my father's adventures, but soon found herself confessing her pains to me.

She had been so young at the time, only 16, when her dad came to see her mother, only she was not home.

"She'll be home soon, if you want to wait?" Ronda told him.

"Sure. Got anything to drink?" He asked, looking inside the refrigerator. Disappointed, he slams the door shut.

Ronda goes back to her room, lays across her bed, grabs her book, and continues to read. As he locks the door behind him, she realizes that he has followed her into her room.

"What are you doing. Go away." She says, but he doesn't listen and she finds herself pinned to the bed by his body.

"Dad, let me up." She struggles.

"Okay. Okay. In a minuet. First, I want to tell you something." He laughs, and she relaxes a little.

"What? Can we sit up, though?" She asks him nervously.

"Sure." He says, sitting up so that she can sit up, too.

"I want to tell you something very important. Just because I am not with your mother anymore, that doesn't change the fact that you are my daughter. Do you understand that?" He asked her.

"Oh dad. I know you're my dad." She sweetly reassures him, patting his cheek. She lets down her guard and moves away from up under him, one leg at a time. He stops her, holding her knee.

"Yes, I know that you know. And you do know that you belong to me, right?" He tells her, looking into her eyes.

Then suddenly, he is ripping off her panties, pinning her down.

Before she can react he has broken in and stolen her innocence.

In her silence, she refuses to tell, but soon she can't hide her belly. She is with child by her own father, and soon she gives birth to Mandie, who would be her only child.

Is Heaven Big Enough for Both of Us?

Lucia is beside herself with anger and decides to move to Los Angeles and take Judy, Billy and the little Mandie with her.

They leave New York City and Ronda, the whore, behind.

It would be years before Ronda would be able to get to Los Angeles and find her Mandie. When she does finally find her baby, Mandie thinks that she is the "Aunt" that everyone has talked so badly about, not her mother. It couldn't be.

Well for years they battled over who was really Mandie's mother. Mandie didn't know what to think. Everyone blamed her.

"She's really a mess." Is what they told me.

"We've really tried to mess her up." Was what they meant.

Well, I met her. I liked her instantly. We bonded over a joint in her bathroom on Easter Sunday 1980. That meeting was ordered of God.

It would be a long time forgotten. But God knows what He is doing. I had no idea it would be ten years before I would see her again. I liked her.

I got a call that night from my dad. He wanted to fill me in on the latest news about Patrick. Yes, Patrick was in the news again.

He had made several attempts to escape, but this one involved guns that he got behind bars. He was able to take over the prison using guards as human shields. He then killed two more inmates.

"He held a makeshift knife to another cell-mate's throat, and made him renounce God." Dad told me in disbelief.

I guess, he pled guilty to a lesser charges in the jail shoot out, and got sentenced to 92 additional years in prison.

"He was sentenced to death for killing J.J. Nobles, too. He's appealing." Dad continued, trying to reassure me. "Gina, I do believe that it is safe for you to come back to Las Vegas."

Safe? I don't know about that.

I stayed with Grandma for a little while until she just got too sick and then we both moved in with Aunt Ronda.

It amazed me that after all that her mother had done to her, Aunt Ronda was still willing to take care of her mom, when she needed help. But, there was still a lot of unresolved bitterness between the siblings.

I had front row seats to the most intriguing display of greed that I had ever witnessed. It was truly unbelievable.

Aunt Ronda felt that because she was now the only one taking care of Grandma, she should be the only one to get an inheritance.

G.L. Johnson

So she talked Grandma into writing everyone but her and her husband out of Grandma's will. Aunt Ronda was now the only heir. It seemed to help her craving to get even with the family.

What about the 75 some years before Grandma got sick? And what made her think that she was the only one worthy to be called an heir? She broke a lot of hearts with her bitterness and greed.

It was sad to see what greed and vengeance can do to a person. Greed was able to turn my Aunt into such a selfish person, so much that no one's feelings mattered. Only hers, and her opinions, and what she thought that they deserved.

"If it were up to me, they wouldn't get a nickel." She said to me, as if it were not my own father that she was talking about, as well as my inheritance. It was so sad. I decided to move on once again.

Back to Las Vegas. Only this time I would get a real job and do things right. Dad got me a job dealing blackjack in a casino where I learned how to deal cards, and, I soon became one of the top dealers at the Horseshoe, where there were "No limits." I spent the next four years raping pockets. It wasn't long before Dad called again with more news about Patrick.

You won't believe it, but, Patrick had just made another attempt to escape from Carson City prison. This time, he was armed as he took 11 hostages, including a female nurse. He was successful for a short time, but they then captured him and returned him to prison.

He had been sentenced to death, but the sentence was reversed by appeals and a new trial has been ordered.

This time his brother Kenneth tells of the torture that Patrick has endured, some of the same stories that Patrick had shared with me that night that we had talked, not so long ago.

The jury listened as the lawyers fought over the life of a man who had been so misunderstood, deciding whether he deserved to live or die.

Patrick was being judged by his peers, but which of them, if any, had lived as he had been forced to live. I thought to myself, were they really his peers, or a dozen of people who could not relate. They probably could not find 12 people who had been tied to a flagpole, or raped by a boss.

Suddenly, I didn't feel so safe in Las Vegas. Maybe I should move.

Nine months later a second jury of his peers, convicts Patrick of murdering J.J. Nobles and sentences him to death by lethal injection.

I prayed for Patrick. He needs Jesus more than anyone that I have met. I am grateful that I met up with him. Someday I would like to thank him for showing me that if you call on Jesus, he will save you.

Ironically enough, in his attempt to make us believe that there was no God, he was able to convince me, beyond a shadow of a doubt, that Jesus is not only real, but He is alive as well. He even loves Patrick. Imagine that.

Dad and I had become really good friends. I had forgiven him for his mistakes and tried to understand his pain. Since, I now knew what had happened in his youth to make him think that it was his right to touch me, I understood. His father had twisted his thinking just like his grandfather had twisted his father's. Poor guy.

In all of the wrong done, the worst was me not telling anyone.

"Why didn't you worn me?" My baby sister asked. "Why didn't you let me know that he was sick and that I should stay away from him."

"I'm so sorry. I should have told. Next time, I'll tell." I said.

"Next time, too late." She cried as she told me of her abuse. Why hadn't I told her to stay away? If only I would have spoken out, I could have saved my baby sister from so much pain.

"How dare she tell." Dad yelled as he foamed at the mouth. "She had no right to tell. I didn't do anything wrong. She did."

He was so angry with her for telling "their secret" that he wrote her off as a traitor. She did far worse than he, by telling.

So I shut up again and went to work at the casino. Alcohol helped me to deal with the pain.

While learning to deal blackjack, I made friends with a couple guys from Jersey. They dealt craps, dice at the Lady Luck. Lou and Phil.

I fell for Phil. He was awesome. Italian. What a babe. I just loved the way he walked and talked, if it could have only been that simple. I was afraid to trust Phil, afraid to get to close, but I was crazy about him.

Lou had a girl named Sandi. A tough little cookie. I thought the world of her and still do. We became best of friends, and all lived together for a little while, but I didn't feel right about it. And there was one major issue.

I found out that the guys had a heroin habit, and showing no mercy, I moved out, and judged them, foolishly.

I learned two very important lessons that year.

The first was judging. After judging my friends as addicts I became pretty self righteous, thinking that I was better than an addict, and before long I found myself addicted to cocaine. I was strung out big time. For over a year, I did at least a gram every day, paying out more than $50,000.

You really can't tell who's doing coke around you. I still maintained a good job and was successful in the eyes of so many people. My boss partied with me, so my drug use was acceptable.

One night, at a "friend's" house, I was offered to "smoke a little."

"Sure. Why not?" I excused myself after every hit and went to the bathroom and puked. About the fifth time I looked in the mirror.

"What are you trying to do? Kill yourself?" Realizing that I hadn't prayed for sometime, I prayed. "Jesus, help me!"

"I'm here. I've been here all along, waiting for you." He said.

I left Vegas in a day and never touched cocaine again.

Another lesson under my belt. No judging.

"This time, Lord, this time. I want to serve you. I know you didn't save me without good reason. I know you have a plan. Help me to follow your plan for my life." I prayed.

Instead of going to Bible College, I went to Street School of Hard Knocks. Either way, you can still learn God's ways. But the second lesson was much more painful to a lot more people.

I had slowly been learning about the power that God has placed in man's tongue. I was about to learn the responsibility that goes with that power.

Satan wants you to believe it is him with the power, but that is a lie from Hell. Satan was stripped of his power and cast down to earth to deceive you into giving him your power.

It is you with the power in your mouth to bless and to curse, and Satan does all that he can to get you to pronounce your own curses. On purpose or not, with your mouth you serve God or Satan.

Sandi and I had become really good friends, best friends in fact. As mixed up as I was I still talked about God a lot.

One day, all righteous and holy, I announced to Sandi, who was about 7 months pregnant at the time, that I had a revelation and would no longer smoke pot with her.

"After all, how would I feel if your baby is born without a foot?" I asked, not even considering the pain that it could cause.

She couldn't believe I had said that. I said that I was sorry and that I didn't mean to be so harsh.

But Lou and Sandi still loved me, and I forgot about the conversation until the phone rang two months later.

"Gina." It was Lou. "We have a beautiful boy." Then his voice broke as he cried. "Gina, he only has one arm. Oh Gina, why?"

"Oh my God, Lou, I'm so sorry." But how could sorry help?

I had not only hurt the two people that I loved the most in this world, but also their son. I had driven a wedge between Lou and God that only God could remove. And with my harsh mouth, I wounded my friends.

Sandi tried to explain to me that the medication that her mother had taken before she was born, had caused the birth defect. But that did not matter to me as much as the words I had spoken to my friend. I would have to live with the memory of a loose tongue for the rest of my life.

"Sandi, I am so sorry. I am so sorry." Was all I could say. Lesson two: Keep your big mouth shut. That's when I found this in the bible:

"Tell them, <u>as surely as I live</u>, says the Lord, what you have said in my hearing, I will do to you." Numbers 14:28

It doesn't matter whether you believe it or not. The word of God will not fall to the ground. Things will happen the way God says that they will happen, and not the way that we want. Do not curse yourself or the people that you love with your tongue. Speak only words that will bless and lift up the ones that you love. We will be held accountable for every idle word that we speak, so you must guard your words?

So, there I stood looking in the mirror.

"What are you trying to do, kill yourself?"

Realizing that I hadn't prayed for sometime, I prayed.

"Jesus, help me!"

"I'm here. I've been here all along, waiting for you." He said.

I left Vegas in a day and never touched cocaine again.

My search continued. What was I searching for? Another school? Another lesson to learn? Or was I just searching for a place to call home?

Call it school, call it home, I call it Hollywood.

Chapter Six
Hollywood

So, as I try to leave Las Vegas, and all of the "stuff" behind me, my "new" boyfriend, whom I was going out with more for sympathy than love, and whom I was also trying to leave, begs me to let him come.

For some reason, feeling obligated to help, I said,

"Get in." Silently screaming, "Get out."

I didn't know how I was going to explain to Vicky what he was doing with me, because, when I had asked her if I could stay with her upon my arrival into town, she gave direct orders.

"No Carl!" I had agreed.

Now as I looked at his pathetic self, I thought,

"She'll understand."

She didn't. She put up with him as long as she could, then nicely, this time, asked us to leave.

So, we got a motel room at The Ocean Park Motel, and we were soon asked to be the Motel Managers. We accepted the job, and moved into a tiny little room off of the office, beginning a 24-hr commitment.

It was awful. It turned out that the owner was extremely evil and was trying to take advantage of the tenants. The rooms were bug infested and filthy, and he refused to fix anything. The motel was close to the beach, so he was able to ask top dollar, and refused a refund when the customer was unable to stay in the room, because of the smells.

With him being new to America and not knowing how nice Americans like to live, I was embarrassed to represent his motel.

Eventually, we helped to close him down and run him out of town, and he wound up having to give everyone back $1,000 each.

We were pleasantly surprised with a $1,500 payment.

That was exactly what we needed as down payment to get into a nice one bedroom apartment in Hollywood at the top end of Laurel Canyon Road. My dreams were all coming true.

I had landed a really good waitress job at Ben Franks on Sunset Boulevard, one of the most popular restaurants in Beverly Hills.

G.L. Johnson

    I waited on the stars as well as the want to be stars, meeting quite a few people who dreamed of fame and fortune. I was just where I wanted to be.
    I felt like a Hollywood star.
    But then, one day, the strangest thing happened.
    Carl brought home a little scroll in a box and put it on the wall and informed me that he was now a Buddhist. We would be going to Temple for meetings. We would be chanting to Buddha.
    "There are many paths that lead to enlightenment." he started,
    "You mean that lead to hell, and you are on ONE of them."
    Where ever he was intending to go on this path, he was the "Man" of the house, and he definitely did need enlightened.
    What was I thinking? Actually, I wasn't thinking and that was the problem. So I went to Temple to learn how to be a good Buddhist, because that was what would bring us success.
    "You must blank out your mind while chanting these words. Only think of the things in life that you want, and that will bring you peace." They taught us
    "What is it that you are chanting?" I asked.
    "It is like a prayer to the universe." They explained.
    "Well, I really shouldn't blank out my mind when I pray. Would it be okay to picture Jesus?" I continued with my questioning.
    "No, there is no Jesus. This practice teaches you to become the highest level of being. You must become the Buddha."
    That was enough for me. Them too. They walked me to the front door and asked me not to return.
    "My pleasure." I assured them not too upset.
    It seemed like, getting kicked out of church, must run in my family.
    Carl changed after that and soon he had no problem getting physical with me when ever we would disagree.
    One day, after announcing that he was going to Japan to sing at a club for six months, I asked him if he had an extra ticket for me. Why not? I had supported his ass while he had struggled for work as a singer. Why shouldn't I get to go, too.
    He punched me. Square in the cheek. Pow.
    "Never mind." I thought, picking myself up off of the floor.
    "Wow, what happened." Lisa asked, when she saw my face.
    "I fell and hit my face on the corner of the desk." I lied.

Is Heaven Big Enough for Both of Us?

She knew that I had lied and waited until Carl's plane took off, helping me to move out of my dream Hollywood apartment to Whittier, where he would not be able to find me. I left my favorite job, as well.

But when Carl got back, he did find me, and talked me into letting him move in again. He didn't have anywhere else to go.

"Please. I'll only be back a little while. Gina, I'm sorry."

I let him move in and he was nice for a while. He started singing on cruise ships, so he wasn't home much. And then, when I caught him in another affair, he offered to take me on a cruise, to make it up to me.

I accepted. Hey, it was a cruise. A seven days and nights cruise.

Carl explained to me that he had told the captain that I was his fiancé, and so, the captain had given us his quarters for the cruise.

I needed to act like we were in love in front of the others, but in the cabin, I was free to not be. I was a good actress, so this could be fun.

The ship set sail. Carl took the week off, this cruise was for us. We partied until late and then we went to our cabin. There was champagne waiting. We toasted our make believe marriage and climbed into bed. I was tired so, I closed my eyes to sleep.

"Gina? You do know that I love you? I never meant to hurt you. Can we try again? Please? Oh, Gina, I want you."

I didn't want to try again. He had cheated on me at least twice and hit me more than half a dozen times.

I was done with the abuse and I was not going to fall for his sorrys

"No, Carl, no." I answered as he slipped his head under my nightgown. "No, Carl, no." I continued, protesting. "No, Carl."

We spent most of the cruise in the cabin. I would give him one more chance. When the ship docked, we were "together" again.

Soon the phone rang. Carl was booked to sing in Japan.

"No you can't go, so don't ask." He glared as he told me.

I wondered why he was so defensive about his Japanese trips. I didn't want to think about it then, I would think about it later. I kissed him goodbye, and he left. He would be gone six months. Just long enough for me to get on with my life, before he would come back and try to screw it up again. What a cycle.

Six months went by much too fast and Carl returned home mad. I was losing all hope in our relationship, ready to move on, and as he went on with his story, I thought that I was in a nightmare with a man that had no concept of reality. He had lost his mind, and lost it over a girl, too.

While in Japan, he had fallen in love with a call girl from Brazil, who, when he told her that he would be leaving to go back to America, killed herself, right in front of him. She jumped out of the window that they were standing next to. She had lost all hope when he told her goodbye. She didn't want to live without him.

It was very sad, but I was very angry and wanted him out. There was no doubt about it, I definitely did not feel the same way about him that she did.

So, as he knelt in front of the Gohonzon, I began to pack his things, to help hurry his departure.

He rose up and I about wet my pants. He had a demon on or in him that caused me to fear. He took a swing at me, and I fell onto my back trying to miss his next kick.

"WACK"

He kicked me so hard in the leg that I heard it crack. I tried to stand up, but I fainted from the pain.

When I came to, he was gone. I called a friend for help and he took me to the hospital where I was informed that there was no way a man could have kicked me.

"It had to be a horse or a jack ass." The doctor said.

I told him that I agreed completely, as they put a cast on it and instructed me to stay off my leg for at least six weeks. I had done it again. I got myself into trouble and needed Jesus to get me out.

"Jesus, I can't wait six weeks. I need to be out of this apartment before Carl gets back from his weekend gig." I cried.

He was booked to sing on a cruise ship for three days. I knew that he wouldn't be able to stop me from Ensenada, Mexico.

So, as I waited for him to go, I wrote a little song in my mind, to remind me of our time together. It went like this:

She smiled and she waved as she bid him ado
As she lay on the couch in a cast.
As the ship "set sail", she jumped to her feet,
Making a move to be free at long last.
No never again, no never again.
He had made it to the top of the list.
"You'll never touch me again."
She vowed with a smile,
Disappearing into the mist.

Is Heaven Big Enough for Both of Us?

And that was exactly what I intended to do. Disappear as soon as he walked out the door. Ready, set, go, and I felt no pain.

I didn't have six weeks to heal but only a couple of hours.

I moved, and I never looked back. One month later our apartment in Whittier was knocked down and nearly leveled by an earthquake. I got out just in time.

I stayed at my friend's apartment for a couple days. And when Vicky found out I had left Carl, she offered me a place with her.

We became friends and I really enjoyed her company. Then the apartment across the hall opened up, so I moved in.

I got a job, working in Motion Picture Production, and soon I landed a gig working for the President of the American Film Market doing his scheduling, and anyone who wanted to see him had to make an appointment through me. I met top film producers.

I remember taking a friend with me to the Grand Party for the opening of the Market. It was totally incredible. What a lay out.

An airport hanger had been converted into an indoor festival.

It was quite a bash. No expense spared. And the food. There was every type of food that I knew existed and more. They even had an oyster bar. But, I didn't eat. Actually, I had lost 125 pounds since my first trip to Vegas and wasn't going to get fat again. So instead of eating, I danced.

"Gina, dance with me." It was my favorite producer. We had become good friends during the production of Wild Orchid.

"You guys back? How was Brazil?" I was excited to know.

"I wish you could have come. It was gorgeous. Here I brought you something." He said as he handed me a box with a beautiful tiny pair of glass ear rings.

"Oh, they're beautiful. Thank you." I said, kissing his cheek.

"Thank you for all your work." He said, "You were right, too. She would have never worked. You have quite an eye for talent."

"Thanks, boss." I said. I loved being part of creating movies.

The next day a Brazilian producers came by and asked me for my phone number, sneaking a quick kiss. I had caught his eye at the party. He was gorgeous, and I had caught his eye.

"You know he's worth 91 million dollars." My boss said.

"No way! Bet he doesn't call." I joked.

That night, my girlfriend, Nina and I sat up late talking. She used to come over after her kids were in bed.

G.L. Johnson

We were good friends. I told her all about the fine week I was having at the Film Market, and how close I had been to a "91-million-dollar man". We laughed at how silly I would have acted.

She went home and I climbed in bed, a little sad, and moments later, the phone rang. I must have just dropped off to sleep, cause I was groggy. It was him. He called! Prince charming called.

I told him that I had already gone to bed, but maybe another time. He said "okay" but that he would be going back to Brazil the next day. My timing was off, and I never heard from him again.

So I guess he couldn't have been my one true love. I mean, if he can live without me then he isn't my destiny. I have got to matter so much more than going home. I just want my man to feel like without me something is missing. There is something essential that I am looking for. He will be someone who wouldn't be complete without me. He's out there and I'm counting on a real miracle to bring us together.

At the end of that week the market wrapped up along with my job and my "91- million dollar man." Well, at least he didn't hit me.

With my connections, I was sure to get into a good production house. I was excited to move on. This was my dream. To make movies. And here I was in the middle of my dreams coming true.

But, Vicky had a dream of managing Rock Bands, so I tagged along to keep her company. Not to mention the wild band parties.

Then she asked me if I would help her in her home office.

She had been working about six months on her own and could use some major help, and I really wanted to see her succeed, so I was glad to help. I had a gift of organization, so I organized everything. Before long I was caught up in her dream, and it didn't take long before I felt like I was doing all the work and getting none of the credit.

I decided to do the same thing on my own, branching off, I got my own band. I stabbed my sister in the back for a little money and a little more prestige, not to mention the contacts that I took.

I wound up hurting Vicky and destroying our relationship because I was thinking of myself first.

I found myself promoting hard core Heavy Metal Bands. I hated the music, it sickened me, the way they exploited women, but I did want to see the guys fulfill their dreams. So, I worked hard to get my band on TV and two days after their album came out they were #6 on the chart. The next day they moved to #2.

The future of the band looked good, and I was a success, but it was at the expense of my sister. I had stolen her idea, which was her heart. There was no joy in it, but lots of money.

Although I continued to share Jesus with anyone who would listen, they served a different god and proudly.

About the same time that I was falling out with Vicky, my cousin Mandie came back into my life.

She had been through so much. The IRS had taken her beautiful home. Her family was fighting and she was very sick. She had a huge hole in the middle of her back where the flesh was being eaten away. She was living under a "curse".

Mandie told me how she had been practicing as a channel in the New Age Movement. She was letting spirits come into her and talk through her, and not seeing the harm in it, she was renting a room to a witch.

We decided to go out and get pizza while we caught up on each other's lives. We got along great. There was an awesome bond between us. We wished that we had been in each other's lives years ago.

Talking for hours, I told her all about my experiences with Jesus, and how he had been there when I needed him.

"He'll help you, too, if you want Him to." I told her.

"I want Him to." She said.

With all that she knew, added to what I knew, and lots of help from God, we uncovered Satan's plan to destroy us.

Mandie gave her life to Jesus in that pizza shop. Jesus had brought us back together just in time.

"So, how's Anna doing." Mandie asked me over pizza.

"Oh my goodness. I can't believe you brought her up. I just talked to her yesterday. She's doing really good, living in Ohio, she just got saved. And she has this new guy, named Max. I guess she thinks he's pretty awesome. She just sent me a video about Satan worship and Heavy Metal Bands. It should be here in a couple of days. Do you want to come over and watch it?" I asked.

"Let me know when you get it. I'll be there." She agreed.

We sat there stunned watching the band that I worked for on this video, while one of the guys in the band sat at my computer. He was a little surprised, too. What was this all about? Did he really worship Satan?

He called a few friends to let them know what I was watching. Then, he tried convincing me that it was just an act for publicity.

You see, I was getting $5,000 a month per band. That's a big blinder. I lived in a 3-bedroom penthouse that overlooked Warner Brother Studios in Burbank, California. What a view. Everything inside was off-white except the fireplace and coffee table. They were made of mirrors. The place was laid out. I had only dreamt of this, and it only cost $1100 a month.

I did not want to believe anything except that it was an act, so I didn't say anything and the guys went on tour.

I invited the lead singer's girlfriend over for tea. I had met her for the first time, at the video shoot. She was hot. Auburn hair and long legs. She was built tight and dressed in black leather straps. The straps barely covered anything. Her role was to lay on the table and "act" like she was having sex with the lead singer. She was powerfully sexy and very believable as she did her horizontal dance. This would be an easy sell.

She showed up for tea and we were soon deep into our conversation when she admitted to me that she was a witch, bragging about how good she was at making blood pancakes.

"They're so easy to make. I'll show you." She offered, smiling. "All we need is a little blood. . ." She boasted.

"No thanks. I don't want to make blood pancakes." I told her.

She laughed. I just wondered why she had to use her gift of beauty for Satan. I looked back at the last six months.

Although I had made the choice to ignore all the signs, they were there. I had spent the last six months working for Satan Worshipers.

I can remember my first meeting with Gene. It was at the video shoot. You see, he wanted me to work for one of his bands. He would be paying me to promote this band. I did not want to go, but I wanted to prove to Vicky that I could get my own band to work for, so I went. I had a monstrous warning from inside that I should stay away, but when I saw him, I thought that he didn't look that 'bad.'

He was wearing an ivory wool sweater, like a lamb, and no makeup.

So, I ignored all the warnings that rose up from inside of me, and I sold out to evil for $10,000 down and $5,000 a month.

I closed my eyes and got on the plane. I was meeting up with the band on tour, in Kalamazoo and continuing on to Washington. I planned promotional events so that the fans could meet the band. We called them "meet and greet" parties. But my insides were freaking out. I knew too much about the evil behind the smiling faces. It was like I was leading children to the slaughter. Giving them passes to Hell.

Is Heaven Big Enough for Both of Us?

"Oh Jesus, what have I done?" Here I was working the dark side. I had wanted so much to serve Jesus, but here I was with Satan worshippers.

Then I realized that I had shared my story and Jesus with many of the people in Satan's little kingdom. Nameless faces began to pass before me, faces of the innocent, that had gotten caught up in Satan worship. I had gotten to share Jesus with a lot of them. I remember how some had listened, so happy to know that Jesus was real.

I began to sense trouble. Fear. No, fear not. I represented Jesus, so I couldn't just run. Or, could I?

I got on the tour bus after the show in New York City. As the band piled on the bus, I felt uneasy. They went straight to the room in back. I sat in the front, alone looking down the row of bunks at the backdoor.

"Get off the bus." It was Jesus.

"Now?" I said. "I'll get off in Washington. After all, that's where my plane is leaving from." So I sat there.

"Get off the bus, Now!" Jesus yelled.

"I'll get off here." I said to the driver, just as he pulled up to a red light. I stood up, grabbing my bags thinking, "Thank God I only have two bags."

As I got off the bus, I ran into the very man that I had met with earlier that same day regarding promoting his band. They are a well known satanic, evil band. I freaked, ready to dart past him.

"I can take you to the bus station." He said to my surprise.

"Don't be afraid." I heard Jesus say. "Breathe."

On the way to the bus station, I told him about how Jesus had saved me from Patrick McKenna. He was quite impressed, but much more so that Jesus was saving me from evil on this very day. He found it especially hard to believe that he was helping me.

After buying me a ticket to Washington, he handed me some money. And as I boarded the bus, I turned around to say goodbye, but he was gone.

I was in Washington in just a couple hours. I grabbed a cab to the airport. I had no problem getting an early flight, and in no time at all I was on my way home. I felt an urgency to get home.

Home? Where was home?

Chapter Seven
Deliver Us From Evil?

"Mandie, do you still want to rent out your spare room? But, don't tell anyone where I am. Don't even tell them that you know me!" I suggested.

Mandie was the only person in my life that I felt I could trust. We had been spending a lot of time together since I had started working on my own and we were becoming very close. I was still not quite prepared for the lessons that we were about to learn.

I moved out of my beautiful penthouse suite into a little tiny 3rd bedroom. It took me a little less than 4 hours to sell or give away everything I owned. I was leaving the dark side and didn't want any stuff holding me back, so I moved into Mandie's with my clothes, my bible, my computer, and my golf clubs.

We got a book by Rebecca Brown called, "He Came to Set the Captives Free" and decided to read it out loud, together.

At the beginning of the book there is a warning that Satan does not want us to know what is in this book and that he would try to stop us.

We shrugged and went on. There was a note about anointing your house and there was a prayer that you would need if any weird stuff started happening. Since we had just found out that Satan Worship was real, we decided to anoint her house.

Then, we settled down into our comfy little couches. We were well into the book, amazed that we had done so many things in our lives in service of Satan. I had no idea. All the time I thought that I had been serving and following Jesus, I had been doing things that were an awful abomination.

I cried in horror. How could I have been so stupid? Satan is such a liar. From the beginning of my life I had been taught that lies were truths. And evil was good. I was not only taught to sin, but the art of sinning.

Rebecca's book revealed a lot of things to me that Satan uses, deceptive tools that we think are harmless.

I found out that everything you do in the occult or sex arena, comes with a demon. You let demons into your life and your body when you bow to Satan. I had lots of demons in my life. That's when I found in the bible the verse that says, *"Now when Jesus was risen early the first day of the week, he appeared first to Mary Magdalene, out of whom he had cast seven devils."* Mark 16:9

"Hey that's me." He appeared first to the prostitute. And I was sure he was about to cast out at least seven devils from me, too!

All of the sudden I was glad that we had anointed Mandie's house. There was a banging on the windows of the room we were sitting in.

It was night, and dark out, so we couldn't see outside the window. The curtains were open about two feet, so I got up to close them, and saw something like a white shadow pass the window.

I gasped for breath, closing the curtains, quickly. I grabbed the oil and threw some at the curtains. I was scared.

"In the name of Jesus, go! In Jesus Name, leave!"

We didn't get any sleep that night. But more importantly, we had not read the deliverance part of the book. Satan had me so full of fear that there was no way I could do what I knew that I needed to do. Cast out the devils that I had let in.

"Submit yourself to God, resist the devil and he will flee." James 4:7

Suddenly I understood. Submit yourself. That's it. I had spent all night fearful of "demons". We had resisted without submission. I should have taken my attention off of the demons and put it on God.

I was ready for tonight. So I thought. We went over our check list as we prepared to be delivered.

Dinner, done. Dishes, done. Hubby, in bed. We sat with our coffee and cigarettes. Yes, coffee and cigarettes.

Now, don't you think that we needed delivered from demons more than coffee and cigarettes?

I found out that it is not the things that go into you that defile you but what comes out of you. Realizing then, that what comes out of you depends on what you've been putting in, I knew that I was full of Satan's junk, and it was time for it to come out.

We began at the top of the list of doorways and temple defiling sins. A doorway is how a demon enters you. Something you did, or got involved with. An open door. So we decided to start at the beginning.

Inheritance: Parents, grandparents, step parents.

Any involvement with the occult, idol worship, demonic infestation, and oaths: Mormon, Masonic, Pagan, and Catholic. Water witching.

We both had catholic backgrounds, as well as pagan. So we began . . .

Is Heaven Big Enough for Both of Us?

"Father, in the name of Jesus, I ask you to cleanse me of any and every thing that I have inherited from my parents."

"In the name of Jesus, I command every demon that came into me by inheritance to leave me now."

That was easy. It is important to use FAITH when you are delivered.

<u>Faith is the absolute acceptance AS FACT that God always performs His word. Always!</u>

So with each declaration the demons had to go.

"If we confess our sins, He is faithful and just to forgive us our sins, and cleanse us from all UN-righteousness." 1 John 1:19.

Well, Satan wasn't going to give up easily.

We hadn't even started on our own sins when the front door slammed. Just then one of those white shadow like things went flying down the hall. I froze. What was it doing in here? It got cold, only we didn't have air conditioning. I felt fear rising up.

"Jesus, what's that thing doing here? I thought that I had anointed." Swoop, swish, it was all over the room, knocked some things over and then went into the antique stand. We sat there for a couple of moments.

"Remember the pigs?" Jesus said. What was he talking about?

"The demons got permission to go into the pigs, someone must have given them permission to be here." I thought to myself.

Demons will cling to antiques, crystal balls, Ouija boards, rock records, tapes, pictures, videos, and idols, even the TV.

We spent the next couple hours getting rid of all the occult objects. Anything we weren't sure of, we anointed.

"Okay, Lord, we're ready, I think."

"You believe that there is one God, you do well: the devils also believe and tremble." James 2:19

I recalled the words of Jesus in my time of terror.

"These signs will follow anyone that believes, In my name will they cast out devils." Mark 16:17

"Look, I give you power to tread on serpents and scorpions, and over all the power of the enemy, and nothing will by any means hurt you."

Luke 10:19

"Come boldly to the throne of Grace and obtain Mercy and find Grace to help in time of need." Hebrews 10:16

This was surely a time of need.

"Thank you Jesus." There was one thing I knew for sure. God's word is God's guarantee. If God said it, it is truth. God is final authority. The moment He speaks, it becomes truth.

God said "Light be." And light was. There is power in the words of God. Put that power to use and stop giving Satan your power by repeating his lies.

"In the way of righteousness is life, and in that pathway, there is no death." Proverbs 12:28

"Let's get this over with." I urged.

Sexual: Sex with opposite sex out of wedlock, same sex, family members, children, animals, and demons. Sadomasochism, and Pornography.

Well, between the two of us . . .

"Father, in the name of Jesus, I ask you to forgive me and cleanse me for the sin of incest with my dad. I thank you for forgiveness. In the name of Jesus, I command every demon that came into me while my dad was raping me to leave me now."

We finished off the list of sexual sins rather smoothly, much to my surprise. Of course, I was wrong to think that we were done with the tough stuff. Most of our sexual sins were done to us. We had been victims. The remaining sins, we had chosen to be involved with.

Just then there was a knock at the door. It was Helena. She was a strange thing. She had brought with her voodoo drums and sage to hang on the door. It was supposed to ward off evil. It was obvious to us Satan was trying to keep us from casting out his pals.

Mandie got sick when Helena started playing her drums, so I told her bluntly that Mandie now served Jesus and if she wanted to visit Mandie, she would have to leave her drums outside. She got mad, made a few remarks, and left, taking her voodoo drums with her. There was the sound of cats fighting and that had me on edge.

"Don't be afraid." It was Jesus.

"Don't be afraid, Mandie. Let's go. I plead the blood of Jesus over this family." My heart was pounding. I knew we needed to finish as soon as possible so I caught my breath and we went on.

Any involvement with the occult:

Here we go. I thought of my involvement with astrology but that was mild compared to what Mandie had tried.

Divination: the art that seeks to foresee or foretell future events or discover hidden knowledge.

Is Heaven Big Enough for Both of Us?

There's palm readings, crystal ball reading, water witching, pendulums, divining rods, tarot cards, tea leaf reading, Numerology, Graph analysis (handwriting), as well as Irid ology (the study of the iris to detect illness). Kinesiology (muscles), Cytotoxology (blood cells), Reflexology, Hypnotism (demons are always placed in a person), Acupuncture, Acupressure, color (for energy levels), and hair analysis.

Astrology, Wizard, Necromancer, Sorcery, and Consoler with familiar spirits, Seances: Ouija board, meditation using spirit guides, and Bloody Mary (a child's game in which children say "Bloody Mary" three times, making demons appear to them)

Divination also includes praying to the Virgin Mary, and encounters with UFOs.

That was a lot of info and we needed to take a break. I went to the kitchen to make some more coffee while Mandie wondered on down the hall to go potty.

I felt something behind me, so I turned around to see Bloody Mary. Screaming, I jumped back and I lost my balance, falling to the floor. Her face hovered over me. I screamed as I freaked out. Mandie came running down the hallway.

"In the name of Jesus, stop. You go now!" She yelled.

We rebuked Bloody Mary and repented for any and all, which were many, childhood games that we had dabbled in.

The face disappeared. I cried, then I cried some more. I wasn't sure if I could go on. Pouring some coffee, I lit a cigarette.

Mandie warned how the next part would probably be the hardest, as she reminded me of how Jesus had always been there for me. She said that God had taken special care to let me know that He would always be there for me.

"There's a reason, Gina, for Jesus to make sure that you know that he is real. He wants you to fight for Him. You need strong faith for what you're being called to do." She said. "If He didn't think you could do it, He would have called someone else. I need your help this time, and next time it'll be someone else, but we do need your help. People all over are giving Satan the right to torment them, and most of them don't even know what they're doing. You have to help. God can use you because of what you have been through." She told me.

It all sounded so nice and spiritual, but I was not ready to hear it. I just wanted to get through the next couple of hours.

"How about some more hot coffee?" I offered.

"I'd love some more." She smiled.

We renounced Satan again. We knew that he didn't want to let go. He wanted to destroy us. But Jesus had other plans.

"For anyone that will call on the name of the Lord will be saved."

Romans 10:13

"Having these promises, let us cleanse ourselves from all filthiness of the flesh and spirit, perfecting holiness in the fear of God."

2 Corinthians 7:1

"Jesus, I know that in Your presence I am safe. I thank you for forgiveness. I will never serve Satan again." I promised.

"All demons that came into me while I was serving Satan must go. You have no more power in my life. In the name of Jesus, Go!" I confessed, prayed, stood, and believed, then continued on.

Occult games and toys: Dungeons and Dragons (witchcraft), role-playing games (visualization), monster toys, cartoons. Martial Arts, Yoga, Eastern Meditation, Visualization, Guided Imagery, ESP, Satanic/Rock music, use of crystals, Astral projection, Blood contracts of any kind. Vegetarianism, New Age Movement, and subliminal tapes.

Murder, violence, suicide attempts, rebellion, drugs & alcohol, inserts (IUD, pins, needles) Blasphemy of God, Occult or Horror movies, and Cannibalism.

There. All the doorways were closed. We sat there, in the living room on the couch, waiting for something to happen.

Mandie was smiling. She looked about ten years younger. There was a peaceful calm in her house and all about us. I smiled back. Before I could say anything, I fell fast asleep.

When I woke up a couple hours later, the sun was shining bright through the window. It was a beautiful day.

Mandie's husband, Jason was at the door.

"I found you a car. A 78 Chevy for $500. It'll get you to Ohio and back." He said.

I knew I had to go. I'd be putting all that I owned into my new used car, and heading east. Heading home.

Home?

Where was home?

Chapter Eight
Mountain Man

As I pulled out of the drive, I knew that I would never be the same again. That was a time that I would never forget. And, I knew for sure that this time was the time for me to finally serve Jesus the right way.

I also knew that I couldn't do it alone. It was time.

As I prepared for my long drive across country, I told Mandie, "Well, I'm off to get me a mountain man." And off I went.

"God's speed!" Mandie yelled.

First stop, Las Vegas. I missed my dad, so a quick visit and then right back on the road. Maybe we can grab a bite to eat, too.

When we got to the restaurant, he grabbed a newspaper and much to my surprise, Patrick was on the front page of the Las Vegas Sun.

This time he was caught in quite an elaborate escape plot. He had burrowed into his ceiling, dug through a reinforced concrete wall, made rope braided from bed-sheets and created masks from papier-mâché and human hair. He also had wire cutters to break through the outer fence. He meant business, this time.

I didn't want to hang out long in Vegas, and really looked forward to getting back on the road. I found myself driving quickly out of Nevada, very soon after my visit with Dad.

It took only four days. I wish I had driven slower. Or maybe stopped more often. I even broke down for half a day, getting a fuel filter in New Mexico. It was beautiful there.

Why did Mandie say "God's speed?"

As I sat at my sister, Anna's kitchen table, we shared are discoveries and adventures. Anna had found God. She had found the One true God. Not the three in one, but the One. Jesus.

I was so happy to see God in her life. I had prayed for my family to get to know Jesus, right after I had gotten saved in Vegas. And I was now seeing it happen.

Of course, since I had been such a bad example, they doubted my salvation. It was hard to tell who I served.

G.L. Johnson

I knew that they didn't believe that I had seen Jesus face to face. But they listened when I explained the trinity. It was quite simple. God is not three in one. God is One. Let me explain.

Since man was made in the image of God, let's start there.

We are taught that Man is spirit, soul, and body.

But we should look at what the bible says.

The bible says that **God breathed His spirit into the body** that He had built to house man. And the **man became a living soul**.

So what we have is the breath of God (spirit) inside the house(body of man) equals a living soul. 1 inside of 1 = 1.

Spirit inside of **body** = **living soul**. Simple.

The bible says that **God is Spirit** and those who worship Him must do it in spirit and in truth. The father is spirit. Not flesh.

The Holy Spirit is God and the body or flesh of God is Jesus. 1 in 1=1. Do you know who you are worshipping?

"Show us the Father." Philip asked.

"Philip, have I been so long with you, and yet you do not know me? He that has seen me has seen the Father." Was Jesus' reply. "My Father and I are one. From now on, you know Him & have seen Him."

"For unto us **a child** is born, unto us a son is given . . .

and His name will be called Wonderful, Counselor, Mighty God, **Everlasting Father**, Prince of Peace." Isaiah 9:6

Isaiah said that Jesus would be called the Everlasting Father.

"In **Him** dwells all the fullness of the Godhead bodily." Colossians 2:9

His titles are Father, Mighty God, Teacher, Friend and Master.

His characteristics are The God who provides, The God who delivers, The God who heals, & The God who comforts.

His NAME is Jesus. The Father has a name and it is Jesus.

Yes, I know who Jesus is, now, I need to find out who Gina is.

Well, Anna soon introduced me to Kevin. He was very handsome. "Red," they called him. We dated for a month. We really liked each other, fought a lot, but that was all we knew. Kevin is very special, and always will be, but he wasn't my mountain man.

In the mean time, I felt like I just had to get a job at the Brown Derby, a local steak house. It kept coming up in my thoughts.

So, finally, I went to apply for a waitress position. I had lots of experience and great references.

After all, I had been a waitress in Beverly Hills.

"I'll take anything." I heard myself say.

What am I saying? Shut up, Gina. No, you won't.

Then I heard myself excepting a position bussing tables for only $2.10 an hour, tips would bring the wage up. Up my__ ,I thought. But I took the job. The first night went smooth. Lots of heavy lifting, lots of cleaning, and lots of sweating, for five hours.

It didn't help when they handed me my tip envelope.

"Thank you Jesus for getting me this job." I opened the envelope hoping for at least a twenty. Seven dollars and sixty cents. Less than a buck from each waitress. What an insult.

"What's up with this, God? I thought that all I needed to do was to 'get a job at Brown Derby?' What are you thinking? I need more money than this, God." I complained.

"Do you trust me?" Was His gentle reply.

"Yes, Jesus, you know I do, I just..."

"Then trust me." He said.

I went to work the next day, thinking about the $3.62 an hour that I had made the night before, with an attitude.

"I'm here, no, no, keep the money, I'll work for free." I said.

I walked into the kitchen, through the swinging doors, and looked up into the eyes of . . . Mountain Man.

"Yes in deed, I will work for free." I thought to myself.

"Now Gina, you do not go potty in the dinner dish." I needed to remind myself of one of the main rules of dating.

"You don't date CO-workers. You always have to leave the job eventually. Besides, I'm just a "bus boy". He probably wants a waitress." Then I added, "But, God, if you can get me this one?"

I passed the "pick up" window, mostly used to pick up food.

"What are you doing for Christmas?" He asked, politely.

I assumed he was hitting on me, so I hit back.

"Partying with you?" I answered with confidence.

"Treat me like a fool, treat me mean and cruel." He sang as he walked toward me. He was cute. I liked him.

He reminded me a little bit of me, and I liked me. He had a great personality and like I said, he was cute. His name, Bobby Johnson.

That night, I gave him a ride home and we talked, and talked, and talked. I really liked him. He said goodnight and as he walked to his door, I watched him from behind. Nice, I thought.

There was only four days till Christmas and I was determined to make him wait for his Christmas present. Me. We got along great.

We both were professional flirts, so we had a lot of fun at work.

Christmas day arrived. He cooked a romantic steak dinner at his place. As I watched him cook, I thought of how nice it would be to marry a chef. I know, I know, it was a little soon to think of marriage, but he was just so cool. He really liked me, too.

After dinner, we watched "Robin Hood Prince of Thieves" and he tried a few of Robin's lines on me. They worked.

"God, I want a baby." He said. What was he saying? This was too serious for me. A baby?

The doctors had told him that he was not going to be able to have children. But he had such a heart for a baby . . .

He would make a good father some day, but not today, I thought. I got a little swept up in the moment and told him that with God all things are possible, especially if two agree.

He was so glad that I gave him hope instead of the "oh wells" that he had gotten in the past.

"You're different from any other girl I've ever met. You make me feel like there is something more to life then before. I feel like I was made for you, Gina, and I found my purpose when I met you. Now, I'm a man on a mission, and I need you to come with me."

We kissed, as we moved closer, and for the first time it didn't feel like having sex, it felt like, making love.

"I want your baby." I whispered in his ear.

I was sick immediately and knew that I was pregnant. But how? He said that he couldn't have children. I knew that I hadn't been with another man, so it had to be his. But how?

"What am I going to do?" I said, looking into the mirror.

"Jesus, how can I be pregnant? Is this your idea of a miracle?"

"As surely as I live, what you have said in my hearing, I will do to you, but don't worry, I have a plan." Jesus answered.

"But he can't have babies, remember." I reminded Jesus.

"He Can't?" Jesus replied. "He can't? Oops." He said.

I guess my only concern would be how to tell Bobby that he could have children. I didn't want to worry, but I was worried.

I knew from experience that men don't always mean what they say. Actually, they usually don't mean what they say.

So, I got ready for work slower than usual. I wanted to call off, run and hide, but I knew that hiding was not the answer.

Is Heaven Big Enough for Both of Us?

How was I going to tell him? I couldn't think of the right way to drop the bomb. When I got to work, he was waiting.

"Gina, I have to talk to you. This might sound a little crazy, but, are you pregnant? I feel like I have morning sickness."

"Yes, we're pregnant." I told him.

I did not expect his reaction. He cried. Then he pampered me and wouldn't let me carry anything too heavy.

At the end of the night I received my first two-week paycheck. After taxes and union dues, two weeks, $32. This was 1991. $32.

"I'll pay you twice that to stay at home." Bobby offered.

"I accept!" I had been so sick that I was thinking of quitting anyway. At least now I'd be getting $64 twice a month.

"You know in Vegas you could get a good job and it costs a lot less to live out there." I told him.

"Give me two months." He said.

I gave him three. I didn't want to rush him since this would be our first experience in the "leave and cleave" dance. Yes, in the bible it says; a man should leave his family and cleave to his wife. I looked forward to being his family. He treated me so fine.

In only six weeks we were in our 78 Chevy ready to go west. We pulled into work, to pick up Bobby's last paycheck, packed and ready to roll. I waited as he ran inside.

"You'll never believe it." Bobby said as he climbed into the car.

He had his money in his hand so I knew that that part was good.

"They closed down. They are moving to Florida." He said.

He had just worked the night before and there had been no mention of the shut down. But, at least they paid him.

We knew we were going in the right direction.

On the way to Las Vegas we made two promises to each other.

1. We promised each other to never believe anything anyone else had to say about us, before coming together, to find the truth.

2. We promised to love each other unconditionally, no matter what we might find out about the other's past.

I never expected the promises to mean as much as they would.

As he drove, I sat back with my eyes closed, thinking to Jesus. I felt His presence in the car and knew that He was still with me.

"Jesus, thank you for Bobby. He makes me feel so safe and so loved and needed. But most of all, he makes me feel cherished. Like I am a treasure that he has found, a treasure that he cherishes.

Smiling inside, I thanked my master, Jesus.

I heard Bobby praying, quietly, asking someone for help. I hoped that it was Jesus. I knew from experience that he could be talking to one of many gods, so I hoped in silence.

"Do you trust me?" Jesus whispered, softly in my ear.

"Yes, Jesus, I still trust you!" I answered.

"Then trust me." He said, gently.

When I woke up, the sun was coming up behind us.

"Let's beat the sun to the West Coast." Bobby grinned, driving like a man on a mission. He turned smiling, "How did you sleep?"

"Can we stop at a bathroom?" I asked.

"Sure. How do you feel? Are you okay?" He pampered.

"I'm great. Everything is perfect." I answered.

He checked the tires as I freshened up. When he finished, he paced as he waited for me to change clothes and brush my teeth. Then I was ready to drive. But, He wouldn't let me drive. He was way to full of excitement to give up control of the gas petal.

We had a blast as we drove on toward Las Vegas, but when we got to the mountains in Colorado there was a blizzard. We had to slow to about 5-10 mph. We still made it into Vegas in 26 hours.

Dad had arranged a complimentary suite at one of the casinos that he was running and began introducing us to his friends.

We celebrated our new life together that night in the hot tub.

"I love you, Gina." Bobby whispered as he held me, as if he never wanted to let go. "You are all my dreams come true."

"This is all so perfect." I whispered as we held on to each other, savoring the moment.

The phone rang, and reluctantly we let go, oh so slowly.

The phone quit ringing just as Bobby reached it.

"Oops, missed it." He laughed.

There was a knock at the door. It was room service. Dad had sent up some food with a note.

"Sorry, I can't make it to dinner but help yourselves to anything you want. It's on the house. We'll get together tomorrow."

"This is all complementary." Bobby asked in amazement.

"Yes, dad signed for everything. He really likes you, Bobby."

Three days later we were moving into our new apartment and Bobby started his new job, and by the end of the month, he was a chef in the Gourmet Room, making double what he had been making in Ohio.

Is Heaven Big Enough for Both of Us?

"Thanks for everything, Sal." Bobby said, shaking dad's hand.

"You are welcome. You know, you are special. Everyone says that you are the best worker in the kitchen. They say good things about you, son. I am proud to be your father-in-law. You can call me dad, if you want. You know that you are just like the son that I always wanted." They really liked each other and that was nice.

"You are too cool, dad, too cool." Bobby told him, passing him the joint. They got along too good, I thought, too good.

Dad went home, next door, and we got cozy in our new home.

I got out my favorite book, and we got ready to set the captive free.

We sat down to read together, and bonded, on a spiritual level, taking turns reading aloud.

Bobby was now on a mission to find out Who his maker was, and Who his master was. I prayed that they were the same?

Chapter Nine
Summer Breeze

"Happy Birthday, babe! What do you want for your birthday?" It was Bobby's birthday. I wanted to give him something special.

"I want to marry you." He did say all the right things.

I thought for a few moments and agreed. Yes, he had won my heart. He was the only one who loved me the way that Jesus did.

Yes, he laid down his life for me and that was all it took. He wanted to do nothing more in life than to make me happy. Was there anything more beautiful than the way that he loved me?

Yes. The way that he loved Jesus.

Bobby had fallen on his knees and given his life to Jesus by the end of Rebecca's book. He had been set free from at least a dozen demons, too. Yes, Bobby, too had been abused and was deeply injured by the people that were supposed to love and protect him. He understood my pain with such compassion that his touch became healing to me. His gentleness won my trust as we became united.

His love for Jesus was so pure and real, and his passion to read the bible and to get to know Jesus blessed me. He had such a hunger for the Lord that it renewed mine and so, we sought after Jesus together, dedicating our little baby, in the womb, to Jesus.

"We give to You, Lord, our first." We prayed in dedication.

Bobby's love for Jesus reminded me of a bible story about two men. One of the men owed fifty dollars to a man named Bill, and the other man owed five hundred dollars to Bill. Bill wrote off both of the debts. Which, do you think loved Bill more?

Probably, it was the man that owed Bill the most.

So it is, that the man who has sinned the most and has been forgiven of the most, that man loves the most, and I knew for sure that I was in the group that had been forgiven of the most. I was a sinner with a capital S.

Bobby and I prayed and studied together everyday.

On our wedding night, we danced to the music from the movie Robin Hood. Bobby held me close as he sang sweetly in my ear.

"Everything I do, I do it for you . . . I'd die for you." He sang.

I stopped dancing for a moment, I didn't like how that sounded.

"I'd much rather you live for me." I whispered.

"Now you've got it." Jesus interrupted.

"Oh, my God?" I said, slowly, as Jesus continued.

"You know how many people say that they would die for Me? But I don't want people to die for Me. I died for them. I breathed my breath into man and said, 'live.' I want people to live for me. I want you to live for Me, Gina. Will you live for me?" He asked.

"Yes, Jesus, I will live for you! Forever!" I said. "I will."

That night I dreamt of a little girl with curly blond hair about two years old. She came up out of my belly. She said that she was my daughter and that she was so glad that I was her mother. She told me how very much she loved me and how she always would. She said that she had a specific purpose and that she wanted only to serve the Lord, and that I must be willing to let her serve Him.

"My name is Summer Breeze." She said.

The next morning I shared my dream with Bobby. He loved the name Summer Breeze, so it was confirmed. This special little girl that God had trusted us with would be named Summer Breeze. I couldn't wait. Neither could Satan.

"What?" I didn't believe them. "Liars." I thought.

It seemed as though I was in a shell and what they said could not penetrate. I refused to believe their lies.

"She has a heart murmur. You'll need to take her to a heart specialist for testing. Take her right away." The doctor told us.

"You are a liar, Satan. My baby is fine." I argued, but reluctantly, I scheduled the first of many appointments with her heart "specialist." She hated going. He pushed this hard, cold, scope against her chest, so that he could see her heart.

"Right there, do you see it?" the doctor asked.

I didn't see it, but Bobby said that he did. I didn't believe him either. All I saw was a perfect little heart. I did not see a hole. But the doctor insisted that it was there, and so I let them talk.

"She will die before she turns one without the surgery."

They wanted to cut open her chest, break open her rib cage, and fix her heart. They wanted to close the hole, and soon.

We prayed and prayed and prayed and prayed. And then we prayed some more. But, we kept getting the same answer.

"Trust me. Trust me. Trust me." Jesus answered over and over. But we kept on praying for an answer. "Trust me" He said.

Is Heaven Big Enough for Both of Us?

We could not put her in man's hands. We had given her to the Lord before she was born and that was who she belonged to. She was safe with Him. I knew that God did not want her to die.

If it was his intention to heal the hole, than he would. I also knew that if he wanted me to let them do the surgery, then he would change my heart to agree with the doctors.

But, neither one of us, had a peace about doing the surgery.

I had read the bible enough to know that sickness was not the will of God. Jesus died so that we wouldn't have to. He bore our sickness. If He bore it than I don't have to. Right?

Jesus told me that He wanted people to live for Him, not die for Him. The same Jesus that saved me, told me to live for Him, and that is what we intended to do. We were determined that Summer Breeze would live for him, too. No matter what the doctors say.

But we didn't know anyone else who believed like us. We started to wonder if we really knew what we knew that we knew.

I sat holding my six-week old angel. There was defiantly something special about Summer Breeze. Her presence was like a breath of fresh air. She was a like piece of God on earth. If only I could get her to eat a little more, and sleep. I sat there holding her.

"Jesus, you won't let her die, will you?" I asked.

Peace flooded the room as He spoke. Softly, gently, he answered.

"I didn't let you die, did I? Do you trust me, Gina?" He asked.

"Yes Jesus, I trust you." I answered.

"Then trust me." He said.

I almost stopped taking Summer to the doctor but I wanted to be a "good mother" and do what the doctor said to do.

At seven months they began to make arrangements for the surgery. I told her doctor that her insurance would be running out soon, so then they decided that they wanted to do the surgery that day.

Bobby and I prayed for the answer.

"Don't you trust me?" Jesus said again.

"Yes, Lord, we trust you." We assured Him.

"Then, trust me." He urged and that made too much sense.

We explained to the doctor that we would not be having the surgery done on Summer Breeze.

He was very upset and said that she might not live passed one and that she would definitely never see her second birthday.

G.L. Johnson

"Jesus, we leave her in your hands, where we know that she is safe. We trust you, Jesus, and I break the curse of the words our doctor has spoken in Jesus' name. She will live in Jesus name."

So, instead of surgery, we opted to go to the beach in California and baptize Summer Breeze in the ocean. We got a room with a view, and went straight down to the beach.

Soon, Summer fell asleep in the cool evening breeze and she looked so peaceful that we decided to let her sleep.

The sun whispered goodnight as it disappeared beyond the water. Lower and lower, until it was gone.

Bobby and I sat there silently, wrapped in each others arms, watching the waves crash to the shore. It was so peaceful.

"That was the most awesome sunset ever." Bobby said as he kissed my neck, smoothing my hair. "Wasn't it?" He asked?

"It was as beautiful as you make me feel." I answered.

His smile disappeared onto my lips. I needed his comfort, so I welcomed his touch.

It was Bobby's birthday, and we had been married a year.

"Happy Birthday, my husband." I whispered in his ear.

"Thank you, Baby, thank you. I am the happiest man alive."

He cried joyfully, as we held each other tight.

How I wished that this vacation could have gone on forever, but it couldn't so we said goodbye to California and headed back to the hot desert of Las Vegas.

"I love the beach." I reminisced.

Bobby had been busy showing me what a good man was all about. He was good. Good at work, good at play, good at everything that I needed him to be good at. He knew how to please me, and that was his main goal.

Bobby was a real treasure, to be cherished.

As the days passed, we found out that we got more than rest on our vacation. We got blessed. I was pregnant, but I already knew it. I felt it that night on the beach.

With Bobby by my side, I could have another baby. He was an awesome father, and as long as we were together, we could do it.

Then came a test of our endurance. We were being put out of our apartment. They had decided to turn the apartments into a parking lot for the casino next door. We'd have to move and soon.

Well, they would just have to wait until after the 16th day of February, because, I was in no shape to move. I was ready to deliver and so I did. Our second little girl was born at 2:30 in the morning. The nurse took her to wash her off and to weigh her. She was perfect. I fell asleep as I waited for my little girl.

Before I knew it, it was dawn. As they brought her to me, I looked out the window as the sun peaked over the Sierra Madras.

Thinking of how it had felt as if I had given birth to a mountain, I named her Sierra Dawn. Yes, she was my little Sierra Dawn.

One week later, the owner of the club Bobby worked in decided to sell. The change at the top trickled down to the kitchen. With much regret, Bobby's boss had to let him go.

Now what? No job, no home. All we had was each other and two little girls to take care of. We moved into a trailer till we thought Sierra was old enough to travel.

We would go East and show our family to our family. Two years in Vegas is more than enough. First we would drive through Colorado and check out the land the Lord had given to us.

So we made plans to give away all our stuff. We knew God would give us more. We met a pastor and his wife who knew of a man who had been homeless with his 5 year-old son.

They brought them over to get what they could use. We gave them everything. They had a complete package for their new home. They began jumping on the beds praising Jesus. We were so blessed. Before leaving, the pastor and his wife prayed with us to receive God's Holy Spirit, and so we did, with joy.

We started on our trip with great excitement, planning on camping across the country.

First stop, Mount Zion, Utah. You have to see Mt. Zion to believe it. Words cannot describe it. It is so beautiful.

I decided to go off alone and talk to Jesus on the mountain side. It was really special here and I felt so close to God.

Jesus told me that he had plans for our family and that Satan was going to try to stop us. He explained that other people's lives depended on us. I kept quiet, listening, and when I went back to camp, I shared all that Jesus had told me with Bobby.

"Guide us daily, Jesus." Bobby prayed.

G.L. Johnson

We got back on the road, headed to Colorado, having a great time, singing and praising God, when suddenly, the car started clanging and banging. It sounded awful.

We pulled into a gas station in Arizona. The report was not good, and I could see the worry attacking Bobby. I was on cloud nine.

"No problem, God is more than enough." I said.

And do you know what else he is? More than prepared.

Bobby paced as the mechanic fumbled under the hood.

"There's nothing I can do. It'll go maybe ten more miles if you're lucky." The mechanic said.

Well, I wasn't depending on luck. I was betting on God to show up and show off, when an Indian woman came over and started talking to me about my babies. We talked a few minuets.

When she heard the mechanic's report, she offered us her yard as a place to put up our tent. She thought that maybe in the morning her husband could take a look at it.

I thanked her as she explained how to get to her house from the station. We crossed the street to get a 2nd opinion, and that report was no better. We decided to try to find the women's house but we couldn't find it.

"Go to the station. She'll come back for us."

Bobby thought that I was crazy until she pulled into the station.

I stayed up and talked with her late into the night. She loved the Lord. I could feel God's presence and knew that all was well.

We finally said goodnight, and I went to join Bobby in the tent. He was crying. I knew God was preparing to do a great work, not only on the car, but on Bobby, so I didn't want to say much.

"Jesus is all around us, baby. Can you feel him?" I asked.

"I just can't believe I brought us out here in the middle of nowhere, and got us stranded." He cried.

"We're not stranded. We are in the palm of God's hand. How much safer could we be? Besides, you didn't bring us here, God did. Do you trust Jesus with your life?" I needed to know.

"Yes, I trust him." He stopped crying and soon was fast asleep. When we woke up the next day you could feel the mercy of God.

God is so awesome. We felt His presence as Bobby and I lay in each others arms watching the sunrise. It was magical.

And then, the girls woke up. The magic faded as we got up to change and feed them. Soon after they ate, both of the girls fell fast asleep. We got busy with our "free" time. It was like magic.

Bobby and Sam, Arlene's husband, went to look at the car while Arlene and I planned breakfast.

I got the steaks out of the cooler, and Arlene added eggs, potatoes, and homemade tortillas. A feast fit for kings and queens. As we gathered around the table we gave thanks for new friends, fine food, and our car.

A bolt had fallen off. A bolt. And Sam had one that fit perfect.

After breakfast, as Bobby packed up the tent, I noticed he looked different. Bobby was learning how to trust. He never had anyone that he could trust before he met Jesus. He looked peaceful.

Sam and Arlene said that they wanted to bless our ministry.

So, I asked Jesus what they meant by our ministry, and He reminded me to tell everyone that He is real. I could do that.

We waved as we pulled away in our 78 Chevy that was running beautifully after its predicted 10 mile life span. We were believing for at least 2,000 more. Next stop, Colorado!

"There it is. It's beautiful." Five acres in the middle of the valley, surrounded by mountains. And one, of them, Mount Blanc is dark blue. It is so beautiful in San Luis Valley.

"Look." Bobby pointed at it.

"This is awesome, God. I surely could live here." I started to picture what our house might look like, but, Bobby felt that God wanted us to go to Ohio first, where, there, He would prepare us.

Ohio? What could we learn there?

Chapter Ten
The Curse Is Broken

It seemed as though we had arrived in Ohio just in time with the message of healing. Both of our mothers had cancer, while Anna was fighting a pseudo tumor, which is a tumor that they can't find but all the symptoms are real, and her husband, Max was suffering with back pain from a spinal problem. The list went on and on.

I knew the answer and was excited to tell everybody the good news. I soon found out how Jesus must have felt when his hometown refused to believe Him. I was shocked at the response. What could I do but stand back and watch them suffer?

Anna and Max were receptive. They not only believed, but they expected Jesus to heal them. They had brains. Why suffer when Jesus has done it for us?

"Jesus, you said that if a believer lays her hands on the sick, the sick will recover. I hold you to your word. I speak health into all the cells in Anna's body, you line up with the word of God that says 'by His stripes we are made whole.' It is finished." I prayed.

"Thanks." Anna said, just before she began a 4-hour puking spell. Anna was sure that she had puked out the tumor, and since she believed that she was healed, Satan wanted to steal her faith.

Faith is stolen by doubt and unbelief. Since Satan wanted her to think that healing was not real, he used someone close.

Anna was very attached to Mom, and with everything in her, she wanted her mother healed. She spent most of her time with Mom, going to Mom's cancer treatments with her. Anna read to Mom from the bible and showed her of Jesus' desire for us to live a long and well life. But my mom didn't believe that she was worthy of God's mercy. She thought that she had been too bad.

But, Anna didn't give up. She pressed in.

I wasn't welcome. They considered me a "Jesus freak" and didn't want to hear my "opinion". I had spent most of my life rejected by my family so this was nothing new. I tried to be supportive of Anna's needs from behind the scenes by supplying the ammo. We kept in close contact for support.

G.L. Johnson

Well, don't you know, God is good! Mom was healed. They didn't understand it, but there was no cancer. Praise Jesus! It was shouting time. But Mom didn't shout. When the doctor told her that they couldn't find the cancer, her reply was simple.

"Oh you'll find it. It's probably hiding behind my liver."

At that point, I wanted to ask her if she had a brain.

Well a little time passed and everyone agreed that it would return. After all, "there is no cure for cancer."

With a confession like that, you can be sure of the results. They found it all right. It was in her bowel causing a block.

There was nothing they could do but make her comfortable. She didn't have much time. I knew that I had to try to talk to her. I couldn't let her die. I headed for her bed.

"Look, the doctors all say that your mother is going to die, so she is going to die." Hunter said. "I don't want you going in there giving her any false hope. Just, please, let her die."

How could I fight with that? After all, he was head of their house. I should just shut up and let her die.

Oh, my God! I can't. I can't just let her die.

"Oh, Mom, please listen to me. Please."

It was not fair that she was never there for me. I hadn't had a mother for the last 15 years. "Mom, please trust me. I'm telling you the truth. You don't have to die."

"Oh, it's the know it all." She replied. She had been in and out of a coma all day, but that didn't stop her from recognizing me. The know it all. I did know one thing, she wasn't going to listen.

"I'm not the know it all, but the know it all does live inside of me." I thought as I left. If only they would listen.

It was time to accept a few things. We were never going to have the relationship that I had hoped for, and Mom was not going to be there for my children, either. I wasn't going back there.

Bobby was so sweet. He is in my life to remove burdens and destroy yokes that come against his family. In other words, he keeps me sane.

Bobby would walk to the hospital after midnight, after we were sure that every one had left for the day, go to Mom's room and sit with her. He anointed her and prayed over her.

We prayed for God, in His mercy to "help her"

I had put off throwing a Birthday Party for Sierra Dawn. She was turning one. We decided to have a small party that Saturday.

Is Heaven Big Enough for Both of Us?

Most of our relatives were at the hospital so we didn't make a big fuss. We put up streamers and balloons and waited for Anna to bring the cake. When she got there, she was a mess.

"Mom's screaming and I don't know what to do. They say that medication isn't working and the doctors can't help. I know it's Sissy's party, but will you please come help, Gina?" Anna cried.

But what could I do? I knew she wouldn't listen. When we got there, she looked awful. I had to do something, but what?

"That's not Mom," I thought. There was a look of torment on her face and she was screaming in horror.

"Jesus, what is this?" I asked.

"Fear has gripped her heart and she doesn't remember Me."

"Jesus, you're here! God, I love you. Help, what should I do?"

"Remind her that I love her. Just remind her." He said.

"Thanks, Jesus." I wrapped my arms around her and started to pet her face. "Mom, it's okay. Jesus loves you. He's right here, Mom. You know Him, you taught me. Jesus wants to take you to heaven. Mom. He loves you, and He forgives you. It's okay, Mom. He's right here" I continued to hold my mother.

"Satan I bind you and your demons from tormenting my mom. You go now, In Jesus name." I demanded.

Then the look on her face changed from terror to peace, and she fell asleep. I continued to hold her just a little longer.

"Jesus, did she do it? Did she call on You? I didn't hear her.

"I did." He said. "Gina, I went to hell for her. She has no place there. Your mother is with me not because she called on me, but because of my sacrifice. You must learn to trust me. I died for all man and nothing will change that. Do you think that you can change what I have finished?"

Jesus explained what He had done for us in a way that I had not yet heard it explained. He said that He did it for us. He wasn't going to take any chances, so He put it all on His blood, His word, and His sacrifice, not on our confession. And, when Jesus said that it was finished because of His sacrifice, there were no stipulations. He did not say,

"It is finished, but now I say to you that if you will change, or if you will do this or that, and he didn't say 'if you will call on my name you will come to heaven . . ."

No, the bible says that anyone that calls on the name of Jesus will be saved. That means made sound, made whole, and delivered from destruction. It does not mean saved from hell. That was done on the cross. It is finished.

Saved in this verse means "right now, help on the spot, saved." It means "call on me and I will save you from the trouble that you are in right now." Your confession will help you here and now, on this earth, not to get into heaven.

No. The last thing Jesus said, as he hung there bleeding, was,

"It is finished." and then He gave up His spirit and went below.

When he returned from the dead he sent His followers out. He gave those that believed in Him power to destroy Satan. Not the power to go to heaven. The heaven part is settled. You need to believe so that you have the power to live a victorious life.

You need to believe so that you have the power to become one of the sons of God. As many as received Him would have that power.

*But as many as received Him, to them He gave power to become the sons of God, even to them that believe **on His Name**."* John 1:10

He did have a point and I would need to think much more about that later, but not now. I hugged my mother once more, telling her goodbye.

"I love you, Mom. I'll see you in Heaven." I whispered.

As I got up from the bed, my aunt suggested that the medicine must be working.

"If only she knew." I thought,

Mom got more than healed that day, she got to meet Jesus face to face. She got to meet the real know it all.

Realizing it was time to quit blaming her for everything that had "gone wrong" in my life, I went home and celebrated Sierra's 1st birthday with my family.

I praised God for giving me two beautiful girls that I could teach all about Jesus.

Then, thanking Jesus that the curse was broken by the power of His blood, I made a promise to my children to honor their walk with God, and to let them be who God has created them to be.

Chapter Eleven
Troublemaker

There was so much going on, with a new family and all, that I had not even noticed the change that was taking place within me. I had begun to develop a fear of people. I suspected everyone, thinking that everyone worshipped the devil and wanted me destroyed, so I was slowly becoming a recluse. I didn't want anything to do with the outside world.

Pain and fear controlled me, so while I stayed home, locked in with my bible, Bobby took care of everything that had to be done outside the house, like shopping or bringing in the mail.

Bobby was my hero, very patiently protecting me from myself. I was learning something very important.

That is that Satan comes only to steal, kill, and destroy. He is the master troublemaker. The closer you are to doing things right, the harder he hits to try to keep you messed up. So, finally realizing who was behind all of my trouble, I quit blaming, my mother, my father, my husband, myself and my God, and I put the blame where it actually belonged. It was time to prepare for war, and this battle is real.

Jesus defeated Satan on the cross, but if Satan can convince you otherwise, then he can defeat you. He wants to stop you, but don't let him steal your life anymore. Put your foot on his head, instead.

I also learned that he'll use anyone who will let him. That includes your husband, your pastor, even you.

I didn't want to serve him in any way.

If you are serving Satan, he doesn't need to try to destroy you or attack you because you are already digging your own grave.

Jesus died for all man. So because of what He did for you, you will go to heaven. But in Revelations, the bible tells us, that evil people will be outside of the gates, gnashing their teeth.

So, you do need to make a choice, that is whether you want to be inside the gates of heaven or outside, gnashing your teeth.

"Jesus?" I whispered.

"Yes, Gina." He whispered back.

"What do I need to do?" I was starting to fear again.

"Trust me. It is finished. I will never leave you or forsake you. And don't forget that My mercy lasts forever. Forever means for ever, and that includes Judgment Day, and forever."

There are two special blessings of Jesus. His Grace and His Mercy.

Grace is God's unearned favor. He gives it to you just because He loves you, not because you have earned it.

<u>Grace is getting what you don't deserve</u>.

Now on the other hand, when everything around looks bad and it's your fault, and you deserve what you're going through, Jesus will deliver you right out of the middle of it all, because of His mercy.

<u>Mercy is not getting what you deserve</u>.

God loves you so much more than you know. It is Satan that hates us. Satan wants to destroy us, but he can't. That doesn't mean he won't try. It means that he can't. There is already an ending. It is written, and the One who wrote the Bible, wins. Get the Bible and learn what God has said about you. Then believe it. Stand on God's promises and do not move. Jesus already won the victory for you. So, now, enjoy being the winner, because the only way that you can lose, is if you are on the losers side. Make the choice and be a winner

You know the saying, "it's darkest just before dawn?" Do you know what it means? It means that right before the new day, the sunshine, right before your dream comes true, it's going to be dark, real dark, darker than any other time, and then, daylight.

Satan will hit you hard to stop you because there is something great just ahead. If he can get you to change your confession or doubt, or give up, he can steal your blessing.

And my confession had changed. We were going through some real growth in our relationship. Which is a nice way of saying, I wanted out. And, what was worse, I was pregnant, again. My hormones had me in quite a state. I was flipped out.

Bobby tried really hard but I didn't. I became demanding, impatient, and mean. I was really pregnant.

Then, when I was six months into the pregnancy we found out we were going to have a son. I didn't care. I knew that Bobby was trying, so I made him try even harder. I was the classic female dog.

Soon, I developed toxemia. So they made arrangements to start labor. Our son was born a month early, so they put him in ICU. They said that his lungs needed more time to develop.

I sat there looking into the little incubator. Jesus spoke.

Is Heaven Big Enough for Both of Us?

"This one is special. He will do great things for me."

"Jesus. I blew it. I've been so mean. Help me change, I want to be a good mother. I just don't know how." I cried.

"Gina, I love you. Don't be afraid." He continued to encourage me. "I think good thoughts of you. Trust me."

"I do." I already felt better. "Thank You, Jesus.

Joshua Thunderstorm Johnson.

He was three days old before we named him. He improved immediately. Within a few hours he was in room air and breathing fine. The doctors were worried that he wouldn't eat, but I knew he would. Not only is he chosen, he's Italian. Eating would not be a problem!

He came home 3 days later to a dysfunctional home. Bobby and I were fighting all the time. The girls handled our mess quite well. I tried to get along but it was hopeless. Then, one day I found the girls in a closet and immediately I thought the worst.

"What are you doing in here?" I asked anxiously.

"Praying." Summer and Sierra echoed.

"Oh, go ahead, sorry." But I stayed by the door to listen.

"Jesus." Summer continued, "Mommy and Daddy need your help. Please help them to stop fighting."

And then, one Sunday, I just didn't feel like fighting. I wanted something else. I told Bobby that I'd be back, and I went searching. I had this supernatural urge to go to church.

"The walls would fall down if I tried!" I laughed.

"I know a church. Turn left here."

"Jesus, are you sure?"

"Trust me. Turn here, up the hill."

As I reached the top of the hill, a sweet presence filled the car, and pulled me toward the front door.

"Jesus, I want a double portion." I put in my request.

"I have some things that I want to teach you. Stay here till I tell you to go." Then he added, "I Am your double portion."

Bobby didn't care that I had found a church or that I was going to change. He wanted out. We had a big fight and he was gone.

But, somehow, I knew that he would be back, and all of the sudden I was back on track to become who God said that I was.

I guess it was time for my head to catch up with my heart.

The first thing I was to learn was that we should put our faith in the power of God and not the wisdom of men. I didn't need a book for that.

G.L. Johnson

The other was that when our praise and thanks equals our asking we would have our victory. I most definitely, might have needed that teaching.

Then a prophecy was spoken out that I just knew was for me.

"The divorce will not go through." The prophet said.

"Thank you, Jesus, for Your mercy and grace." I thought.

We went home and turned on the praise music and never again asked for my husband's return. We prayed a new prayer that night, like this:

"Thank you Jesus, for protecting Daddy while he is away. And thank you for bringing him home safe."

Guess what, Daddy was home by the end of the month.

I learned what it means to only need faith the size of a mustard seed, because that was all that I felt that I had. But it moved a big mountain in my life. He came back in love with me and ready to serve me, and to lay down his life for me, again. I was tripping.

Faith is preached a lot. And it is very important. But you must be careful not to put faith in your faith. Keep your faith in Jesus.

Check yourself during a test. Are you making sure that <u>you</u> are doing all the right things or do you have your mind fixed on Jesus?

Jesus doesn't move for you because of what you are doing, but because he promised you he would.

Do you think that God's character changes because of how you act? He'd be a flake if so. Your actions do not influence God's character. He is a giver, a provider, a healer, your source, whether you are a nice guy, a bully, a jerk or a clown. God is God because of himself, not because of you.

"Quit trying to make it happen and let it happen." I heard Jesus say. "Tell them to quit trying to make it happen and let it happen."

Jesus loves you more than you love him. Set your mind on God and not on yourself or your need.

Bobby came with us to church on Sunday and gave his life back to Jesus after a powerful message about Noah being the only righteous man in all the world. He stayed righteous in the evil day he was living in. Noah didn't have anyone to fellowship with except for God. He was the only one that knew God. Talk about some peer pressure!

Bobby and I decided to take a stand and let God prepare us to handle a double portion of "Christ. The anointed One and His anointing."

I learned that the most important thing I can do is lift up my hands and voice to the Lord, praising him with everything that is in me. I praise him continually. His name is always on my lips.

I am finding that the more I praise Him the more I change. Change is good when you start where I started.

"Jesus, I want to love people again. Give me a hunger to share you with all people. Let me love again." I couldn't believe that I was even asking God for that. Love people? No thanks! How could I love people again?

But as time past, I found myself talking to people again. I wasn't afraid to talk to them anymore and I wasn't afraid to leave my house. I had been delivered from fear. I felt so free.

But being delivered from fear was only the beginning. Love?

Suddenly, I realized that there were many, many people who loved Jesus just as much as I did.

For nearly 20 years, Jesus had only been my God. Most of my friends either didn't believe or served other gods. I had met a few people who claimed to love the Lord, but I had wondered.

Now I faced the realization that I wasn't the only one hearing from God. I realized the importance of each and every person. Not just the saved, but the unsaved. I realized that but for the grace of God, I could be right along side of them.

Jesus died for all of mankind. All means all. Even the people that you don't like, and the people that you don't understand.

That morning, in the Las Vegas Sun, I read that Patrick's third death penalty hearing was scheduled to begin This will be his third jury.

Maybe this jury would be able to understand his pain.

As a security precaution, Patrick will be transported in a wheelchair to and from the Clark County Detention Center in belly chains and ankle shackles. He will wear blinders and his hands will be covered in mittens to prevent him from grasping onto anything. While in court, he will wear a remote-controlled stun belt with a 50,000-volt shock capability to incapacitate him if he tries anything, which he has on several occasions.

With armed swat officers watching his every move, he dare not move, as they stand ready with high powered rifles shouldered.

Security will be tight, and every precaution will be taken.

Officials in Nevada have said that Patrick is the most dangerous man in the state's prison system and the third most dangerous in America.

Saturday August 5, 1996 would start his final stand.

Patrick defended himself, as he pleaded with the jury.

"Please don't let them execute me?" He begged. "They are doing it for the wrong reasons. They are using me as an example because they can not stop me from escaping." He protested accusing prosecutors of wanting to execute him because of the embarrassment he had caused the state by escaping three times as well as planning the most elaborate jail break in Nevada history.

But his own violent past stood as record against him.

County prosecutor, Dan Seaton said it was a "sad truth" that the state was seeking the death penalty, but the sentence was not being sought to spare prison officials further embarrassment, but to protect lives.

"Should the jury give Patrick a life sentence without parole, his solitary confinement could be lifted and he could return to normal prison life, endangering the lives of guards and other prison workers." Seaton said.

Clark County Deputy District Attorney, Doug Herndon fought along side of Seaton to have Patrick executed. He reasoned with the jury.

"You look at all he has done and all he has wrought, and you give him the amount of mercy that he deserves, which I submit, is none." He said. Urging the jury to not accept the "abuse excuse" or shift the responsibility onto abusive parents, he held up a large chart that detailed Patrick's criminal record from birth to the present.

"You are not sentencing a little kid in a cowboy hat from 1955."

Doug added, reminding the jury that the childhood photos were only a minute part of Patrick's history.

A woman then took the stand, and told of a night 18 years ago, when McKenna had taken her to an isolated spot near Lake Tahoe and talked of killing her. She said that he was armed with a pistol that she believed he had used to kill her friend, just moment before.

Tears welled in her eyes as she told how he had stopped the car and walked her into the woods off the Mount Rose Highway to Lake Tahoe, where he took down her pants and began fondling her. She said that she offered to do any thing that he wanted if he would not kill her. She was only 17 years old at the time.

"He told me that I was too young to kill, but held the gun to my head and pulled the hammer back and said that he would kill me if I told the police, even if he went to prison." She cried.

In the end, he neither raped nor shot her. She flagged down a passing car, which took her to the ranger station.

Is Heaven Big Enough for Both of Us?

When authorities arrived at the home of her friend hours later, they found him hog-tied and suffering from an obvious bullet wound to the head. But he did not die from the shot and showed up in the courtroom to testify that McKenna was the man that shot him. When questioned about the incident, he admitted that he remembered nothing.

Judge Leavitt then ruled that the jury could not hear his disjointed story or see how debilitated he is from the shot that damaged his vision, hearing, memory and balance.

The prosecution told of how after being convicted of raping two women in a Las Vegas motel, Patrick returned to his cell and murdered his cell mate J.J. Nobles after J.J. had refused him sex.

The jury had a tough decision ahead of them. Should Patrick be sentence to death by lethal injection or given life in prison with or without the possibility of parole for these crimes.

A psychology professor advised the jury not to give Patrick the death sentence without further investigation of how his abusive childhood may have damaged his mental health.

Professor Stephen Pittel of Berkeley, California said that it was possible that childhood beatings and a brutal and humiliating juvenile detention may have encouraged his aggressive behavior.

"I am not in any way an advocate for Patrick McKenna," Pittel said. But I personally and professionally feel that the jury should have access to that information before passing a verdict on a man's life." He explained.

You see, Patrick had never been evaluated by a psychologist during his more than 30 years in prison.

Pittel added that he was struck by the emotion that McKenna expressed over his daughter's death.

"The ability to feel grief, for a dead child is the best sign of a conscience, and the idea of a grieving and remorseful McKenna clashes with the widely held belief that he is a cold-blooded psychopath." Pittel acknowledged.

Then, two of Patrick's four brothers, Tim, a successful Henderson real estate executive and Ken, the Reno lawyer, testified that their older brother craved their father's love, but never received it.

They recalled one dinner when their father threw spaghetti in Pat's face after learning of his poor grades. He then dragged Patrick outside and began punching him as they watched.

In a tearful plea, Patrick's niece asked that her uncle's life be spared so that her unborn daughter could benefit from his wisdom and love that had helped her through her troubled times.

She told of how "Uncle Pat" was there for her during her stormy first marriage when she was 18. He had encouraged her to move ahead after a painful divorce, and to pursue her dream of an ice-skating career with Disney.

"He has never let any of the family come help him because he thinks we're ashamed of him. I'm not ashamed of him." She said.

She was sobbing, obviously overtaken by the love that she felt for her uncle. She took a deep breath as she continued her plea.

"I just want to ask you not to take him away from me, please. In about four months I am going to bring a little girl into this world and I don't want to bring her to her Uncle Pat's grave site . . .

. . . I don't want to tell her that this wonderful man isn't here to help her through hard times." She cried.

Jurors leaned forward in their seats as she spoke, and Patrick smiled fondly, which drew tears from his family as well as his public defender, Nancy Lemeke.

Tim said that he was grateful that his brother had permitted his family to fight for his life.

"In the past he had not permitted us to testify and had forbidden us from speaking about our violent childhood." Tim admitted.

"Pat does not deserve to be killed by the people who helped create him," Tim's wife, DeEtte protested. "It's kind of like an eraser. If they kill Pat, all their mistakes go away."

McKenna's defense team fought, arguing that their client's volatile family life, abusive juvenile probation officers and the death of his own child helped to trigger his own violence, but they somehow sounded ridiculous with their claims that his victims had deserved to be attacked. After all, look at where they were.

"Some crimes are worse than others, some rapes, some sodomies are worse than others, and those who lived similar lives of crime – such as his victims – invited such violence. . . These were not angels drug into a hellish plot." Argued Peter LaPorta, another of Patrick's public defenders.

Nancy Lemeke, then toyed with the jury's faith as she spoke.

"For these crimes Patrick McKenna will die in Ely State Prison. He will leave in a pine box. The question is 'Will God decide when or will you?" She said before taking her seat, letting Patrick have the final words.

He asked that the jurors bear with his awkwardness because he was out of his element.

"I don't know how to function out here," he said. "I don't understand the values. I don't know how to fight with words."

Patrick told the jury that for more than 30 years he has lived in a world of crime, a place ruled by a code of violence, a place with no room for compassion.

"The people who shared in this world with me accepted the inherent danger. I would never turn my violence on "real people, real citizens. I don't tell you these things to justify my criminal behavior. There can be no justification." Patrick proclaimed, continuing his defense, telling jurors that he shouldered all the blame for those that he had injured, but that they were wrongly seeking the death sentence to keep him from escaping again.

"I don't have the answers, but I do know who is to blame. I blame myself. I blame myself for not having the strength to pull myself out of that life. My remorse, my guilt, my feelings and my shame – that's my humanity. That's what makes me alive. I refuse to give up, for my sake and my family's sake. I am not going to become hate-filled and unfeeling." He said.

Patrick finished his final statements and then he sat down and waited. The trial had lasted only 1 ½ weeks. The jury deliberated for 3 hours on Wednesday and 1 ½ hours on Thursday, before reaching a verdict.

On Sept 19, 1996 a ten-woman, two-man jury of his peers, returned with their verdict.

Although they found that Patrick was physically, mentally and emotionally damaged by his abusive childhood and the loss of his baby girl, they said that it did not outweigh the need for his punishment by death. The third jury ordered his execution by lethal injection.

Patrick closed his eyes as the verdict was read.

Nancy walked out of the courtroom sobbing and crumpled into Tim's arms.

"I'm so sorry." She cried. "I'm so sorry. I just feel sick. He is more concerned for us and how you guys are than for himself."

"No." Tim said. "You did a great job. You just hold your head up. You fought hard, and you did a good job." He assured her.

Tim spoke out, objecting to the decision.

"Pat doesn't want to live in our world." He said. "If he tries to escape, it's a chess game. It's what keeps his mind alive. But to escape and go out and harm anybody?" He shook his head. "No, I wouldn't want Pat as my neighbor, but I do want him alive."

A 50 year old Patrick returned to Ely State Prison where he is likely to remain in solitary until his death sentence is carried out. Execution is set for the week of Dec 9, 1996, but the case will be appealed automatically.

My heart cried for him. I stopped reading and prayed.

"Jesus, please be merciful. Patrick was somehow able, in his hatred and anger, to show me mercy and let me live, show him your mercy, and give him new life. Let him feel Your presence and Your peace. Let him know that You do love him. And, let him know how truly grateful I am that I met him that night in Las Vegas. Let him know that it was him who showed me that You are real. Please thank him for me, and let him know that he is part of Your plan." I prayed for him with all my heart, truly wanting him to feel better. I felt bad for him. My life ain't so bad after all. Isn't it crazy who Jesus can use to reach you?

One day, Regina, a lady that I had met at church, asked us to pray about hooking up with her street ministry that was in Akron.

She would spend her Saturday afternoons sharing the Lord with the homeless and the "less than desirable." She used pizza to draw them in. Pizza. And it worked. The people came.

Regina's heart was to reach young girls before they ended up where I did. And, not having heard any of my testimony, she asked me to come and speak. I was thrilled. I really wanted to make a difference in someone's life.

Tony came back to the Lord. He had simply forgotten Jesus and just needed a reminder. He was minding his own business walking down the street when Bobby approached him.

"What does this guy want." Tony thought, but then he saw Bobby's smile and thought, "I think this guy cares."

So he decided to come and see what was going on inside, and dedicated his life to Jesus. He said that he would not forget Bobby reaching out to him. But the man I will never forget, asked for my prayer.

"Pray with him." It was Jesus.

"I'll get someone." One of the girls ran to find a male pastor.

I just stood there, watching as he was told that God couldn't help him unless he was willing to go to church. He looked devastated. This man didn't even have a home to take a bath. How could he go to church? He tried to state his case, but the pastor threw up his hands and walked away.

Jesus was mad. I knew better than to ignore him.

"Don't you dare let him walk out of here." He said.

"Excuse me, sir. I just want to tell you that God said that He would never leave you or forsake you. Where ever you go, he is with you. You don't have to go to church. God wants to help you right where you are."

"I knew all along that I wanted you to pray with me, will you pray for me to get the Holy Spirit?"

"I would be honored, sir." We joined hands, "Jesus, our source, our father, we come to You asking You to fill Dave with your Holy Spirit. Your word says that You give freely to all that ask, not holding anything against us." We held hands. "We thank You for Your promises. And Jesus, You said that You go to prepare a mansion for us. You didn't say we had to wait to live in it. We receive Dave's mansion. Thank You for caring about our daily needs. You said that you prepare a table for us in the presence of our enemies. We have no enemies in heaven, so You must mean on earth. We receive Dave's table of blessings." I prayed. "Father, You know what Dave needs and I want to thank You for meeting all of his needs, in proportion with Your riches, and in glory, gloriously." I rejoiced, and then, I commanded. "Satan, I bind you. You have no authority here. Dave is a child of the Almighty God. You will bow your knee to the name of his Lord, Jesus." We finished praying and Dave said,

"Thanks!"

I hugged him a said goodbye.

"Thanks!" I heard Jesus softly say, as I walked away.

"No Jesus, Thank you!"

I knew that I wanted to spend the rest of my life telling people that Jesus loves them now, right where they are.

We will never forget Regina. Through her, God showed us that we could be a part of sharing Jesus with the world.

I rejoiced because I could serve the Lord. But more than anything, I rejoiced because I would not be the only one in Heaven, after all.

Chapter Twelve
Is Heaven Big Enough?

"Sunday is communion." Our pastor was reminding us not to miss church on Sunday. "Be sure to check your hearts this weekend to make sure you have forgiven any and all who have offended you. If you take communion and your heart isn't right, you'll be drinking unto damnation."

I looked at Bobby. He looked at me. We would both be checking our hearts. There were so many people who had hurt us in our past, but we knew it was time to deal with it and move on.

The bible says that Jesus was bruised for our iniquities, wounded for our transgressions and by his stripes we are healed.

<u>Iniquities</u> are sins that have been passed down to us that we don't even know are sins. Things we have been trained to do naturally.

<u>Transgressions</u> are when someone steps on your toes or crosses you. Wounds that go deep. But Jesus was wounded for us.

I realized it was time to let Jesus be Jesus. What was I doing feeling the pain that Jesus had taken on for me? I had no right to hold on to my wounds. I made a decision to forgive all who had hurt me. Some of them I would have to forgive in faith, trusting God that my feelings would catch up, but still from this day on they are forgiven.

Forgive means that it never happened. The charges have been dropped. There is no fine.

"Jesus, how can I forgive?" I asked.

"First. Stop picking the scab." He said.

Boy did that make sense. Then he continued.

"Give me the wound and I will supernaturally heal it. Do you remember how I taught you to forgive when I was on the cross. Do you remember what I said? Do you remember how I was able to forgive those who were hurting Me?" He asked.

"Yes, Jesus. You said 'Forgive them for they know not what they do.' but, should I let them off the hook that easy?" I asked.

"I forgave you, that easy." He reminded me.

"You're right. I didn't know what I was doing or I wouldn't have done it. I just know I wouldn't have. If I would have known the right ways to act and the right things to do, I just know that I would have done right." I defended my actions.

"Gina, It doesn't matter what you would have done, I forgave you for what you did do." He assured me.

He went on to explain that forgiveness is not an option. "Forgive, and you will be forgiven." He commanded.

I realized exactly what I had to do, knowing that with God, all things are possible. There is nothing too big for Him. I also realized that it was now up to me. Just how much did I want to be forgiven? Enough to let go of the pain, and the anger and the filth. Enough to forgive? But I needed my anger to help numb the pain.

"Jesus I confess as sin the UN-forgiveness in my life. By faith, I forgive all who have hurt me because I know I must. Heal those relationships, supernaturally. Bring us back together and please, strengthen our love for each other. For those, who don't know you, reveal yourself to them. And, Jesus, for anyone who I have wounded, I ask forgiveness. Help them to forgive me so that their wounds can heal. Thank you for restoration."

I took communion that Sunday with a right heart. As I left church that morning, I had a renewed compassion for my family.

So many things had happened that I wasn't sure that I even wanted to see them again, let alone spend eternity with them. I realized that if I didn't want them in Heaven, that meant that silently I was praying for them to go to Hell. I thought about it and about how selfish I was being, wanting God all to myself. I repented, knowing that only God could have changed my heart.

"Jesus, I do love my family. Please forgive me for being so selfish. Thank you for showing me that Heaven is big enough. And thank you for saving each and every one of my family."

"Gina, I'm glad that you want your family saved. So did I. And I promise you that you and your family are saved. Everything is taken care of. Heaven is big enough!" And for the first time I knew that it was.

"Hello." It was Anna, calling to find out what Summer Breeze wanted for her birthday.

"A dinosaur and a lion! And a party at McD's and I want Grandpa to come." Summer pleaded.

Well Grandpa Hunter came, and watching him talk to Summer, I realized how very blessed that we had been. He had taken care of us and loved us when we were very unlovable. He put up with a lot from me, and he was still around.

All those years I had blamed him for breaking up my parents, but I had been wrong. God had planned them to marry.

When I asked Jesus about the marriage, he said that my brother was not a mistake. It took careful planning to arrange his birth. He would not be who he is with different parents. Had they not met, my brother would not have been born. He wouldn't be who God planned him to be. My brother is living proof.

"I'm sorry Lord for judging my parents lives. They don't have to answer to anyone but you. There are so many things that I don't know. I repent for trying to be you."

"Apologies accepted. And, by the way, about this "drinking unto damnation", how can you drink of Me and be damned? Do I need to say more about that?" Jesus questioned my understanding.

"No. I understand." I said. What a relief.

How can you drink of Jesus and be damned? You can't. So drink of Him and don't worry. Your head and your heart our in the good care of Jesus, and He will not leave you broken or damned.

He didn't leave you out. Heaven is big enough for you, too. I don't care what you have done. Jesus loves you. He died for you, rather than live without you. Just to ensure that you would spend eternity with Him, He did not take any chances. He didn't count on anyone or anything but Himself. He sacrificed Himself, paying the price for you to be redeemed, so that you don't have to go to hell. Payment has been made for you.

Now come on in and experience Love, and Joy, and Peace like the world has never known. And don't worry that you won't be able to live up to it. All mistakes are forgiven. Just run to Jesus instead of from Him.

"It is finished." Jesus said it himself, so you don't have to believe me when I tell you that it is finished. Believe Jesus.

There is nothing that you have done that is bigger than what Jesus did for you on the cross before you were even born. Absolutely nothing can change what Jesus has done. It is finished.

You are not going to hell for anyone or anything, so rejoice.

You don't have to change first, this is a come as you are party. Although, the more you get to know Jesus and the closer you get to understanding who you are, the more you will change.

If you are still not sure where you will end up or where you will spend eternity, read this out loud.

G.L. Johnson

"Jesus, thank you for dying for me. Come into my heart and live big in me. Be Lord of my life. I receive Your Spirit, and I choose to live for You forever."

*But as many as received Him, to them He gave power to become the sons of God, even to them that believe **on His Name**." John 1:10*

Part Two

Triumph: In Spite Of It All

Chapter Thirteen
The Question

*"And His sheep follow Him: for they know His voice.
And a stranger they will not follow, but they will flee from him,
for they know not the voice of a stranger."*
John 10:4-5

As I lie awake wondering what my next move should be, I looked back at the last year.

"Oh, God, was that really you? Or is Satan trying to get me to destroy my life, again. I need to know. If it was you, then give me the strength to stand. If it wasn't you, tell me now, and I'll admit my mistake. I'll tell everyone that I missed it and ask them to forgive me. I wish I had never written that book." I cried as I poured my heart out to God. I was confused and hurt.

"You know, Gina, if they hate the book, just wait till the movie comes out." Was His gentle reply.

Peace rushed in as I laughed. I had not been able to laugh about the situation for some time. Who would have thought that doing what God asked me to do would send me on such an adventure . . .

"What do you mean, write my story?" I knew His voice after all these years, but still . . . "I'm not a writer. And besides, who would read it? Please don't ask me to admit that I have done all those awful things. I don't want to air my laundry outside. What will people think? How will I ever be able to . . . but you are God. If you really think that it could help someone . . . even if I could help one person . . . Okay, I'll do it."

I sat down and began writing, and kept on writing for hours. Done. I went back over it to edit it. Then one more time to proof read it, and then off to the printer.

Bobby sat down to read the first copy. He laughed, then cried, then laughed, then cried. Then he put it down.

"It's good, it's really good." He said.

"Do you really think so?" I asked him. "You know, I'm not a writer. I can hardly believe that I wrote a book. What a trip. I wonder what God wants me to do with it now?"

"Give that lady, over there, a copy." I heard Him say.

"No, God, not her. I'll have to pray about it." I was hoping that I had not heard Him correctly or that I could change His mind, or something. But after much travail and suffering, that I put myself through, I gave her a copy. She was a tough little lady, who had been terribly abused by her husband who was an active Satanist, as well as an Italian Gangster.

She was scared and carrying a lot of guilt from her past. She had a hard look about her and a wall built around her for defense.

"Gina, I read your book. Thank you so much."

She went on to tell me that as she read, she felt the anointing of God and was set free from her past. As I watched her in the next few weeks, I noticed a softness had come over her and the hard pained look was gone.

"Jesus, You were right. I'm sorry for arguing." I told Him.

"I'm used to it. Now, give that lady over there a copy."

"Oh, God, surely you don't want her to read it. I'll pray." Weeks passed. Every time I saw her, I felt guilty, like I needed to obey God. I finally gave in and gave her a copy of my book.

"Gina, I read your book. Thank you so much." She went on to tell me how she had been molested by her father. She had been experiencing so much guilt and UN-forgiveness in her life that she was just miserable. She thought that she was worthless. As she read, she got healed and set free. She, too, looked different.

"Maybe you were right, again, Jesus. Maybe you can use my book to help others." I admitted that I could have been wrong.

I shared it with a few more people and the testimonies started coming in. I was amazed, mostly that God would use someone like me, damaged.

"Gina, could Bobby and you come into the office. We need to talk to you." It was the associate pastor at our local church.

"Wow, Bobby, this could be something good." I said.

"Maybe they want to put it in the bookstore." Bobby hoped.

So into the office we went with our hopes high . . .

Boy, did we miss it. They wanted to tell me that my book was not from God and that I was not to share it with anyone at "their" church. So, I agreed to keep it away from "their" church.

Bobby wasn't so agreeable. He was mad. He said that I should obey God. If God told me to give it to someone, then come what may, I must obey God. He walked out of the office, mad.

But, I didn't want to make waves so I agreed to stop sharing it at church and I began sharing it at work.

Is Heaven Big Enough for Both of Us?

At times, when I'd be walking down the street, God would tell me to give it to someone. Testimonies were pouring in; healing, salvation, and deliverance. I really didn't understand why my pastor was so against it, so I asked him if he had even read it.

"I don't have time for junk like that." He said, shunning me as though I were dirt, as he gave me a look of disgust.

The worship leader, whom I really admired said,

"You can not reveal darkness with darkness."

And that was true, so I asked him if he had read it.

"Parts of it." He said.

How can you understand what the author is saying if taken out of context? Shouldn't you read a book in its entirety to get the real meaning? I guess that he had only read the dark parts. I was sad.

"That is why they don't understand My book." Jesus said. "They jump around instead of reading it from beginning to end.. It is frustrating to have given so much and to have it picked apart and pecked at. A little peck here and a little peck there. Like chickens. I too, wish that they would read it as a completely finished work."

"I will. I do. I have." I defended myself.

"That is why you understand. That is how you know me. You cared enough to want to know me. After all, I am the Word."

One day after church, the associate pastor's wife, pulled me over to the side. She whispered to me, as she confirmed her belief.

"I just wanted to tell you that I can see the anointing on your book and I can see how it could help. Thank you for writing it."

And so I battled daily with Jesus. He would ask me to share my book with a certain person, and I would call Him Satan and tell Him that He could not destroy me. I told Him that I would be no part of His plan. My past was under the blood and I didn't have to ever look at it again.

"They told me to forget my past. It is covered by the blood." I said.

"Gina, listen, if you put a cover on your couch, it is still your couch. Right?" He tried to explain. "Right?" He asked again.

"What are you saying, Jesus?" I wanted to understand, so I listened carefully as He continued.

"Well, if you put a bedcover on your bed, it is still your bed. Your past is covered, but it is still your past. Don't be ashamed. Don't make your past pains worthless by concealing them. You need all that you learned in your past to fulfill your future. Look back at your past and learn from the good and bad. Learn from the right and the wrong choices.

You need all that you have been through to help the ones who you were created to help."

"That is not what the church says." I argued.

"Consider Paul. You know, the Great Apostle Paul. He said to 'forget those things behind us and press on toward the high calling of Christ.' I ask you, how many times did he talk about his past?"

"I have no idea. But I know that he told the chief captain at the temple and King Agrippa. In Acts 22 and 26. So twice I guess."

"He told it six times to every person who has read the bible. He has definitely told more people than you have, so far. But, you see, he needed his past to fulfill his future." Jesus explained.

Yes, it is quite a testimony to have written most of the New Testament, but the real meat of that fact is that he was a mass murderer who enjoyed killing Christians. A serial killer, only commissioned by the government.

"Do you see how much we needed to know his past to really see the power and mercy of God. Just as well, Gina, you need your past to fulfill your future." Jesus explained.

"Fulfill my future? What do You mean?" I questioned. "Do I really have a future? But the church thinks that I'm evil. How can You use me? What could You possibly want me to do that could be so important?" I asked with a real desire to know.

"Give that lady over there a copy of your book." He answered.

"No! I won't do it. Look, my pastor said 'no'. Don't I have to obey him? Isn't it his way or the highway? God help me, please. I want to listen. I want to obey You. Please, tell me what to do?"

"Give that lady over there a copy of your book." He said again.

Well, I didn't give her a copy, even though I knew that Jesus wanted me to, I just couldn't do it. So, Jesus went around me.

"Gina, I read your book. Thank you so much. I gave it to my daughters to read." The lady told me, much to my surprise.

"Where did you get my book?" I demanded an answer.

She told me that one of the ladies, that I had already given a book to, 'felt led' to give her a copy. So she did. You know, I really didn't have a clue. When you hear that God is in control, He really is. And when He wants something done, He'll get it done, with or without you. I had been disobedient to my Lord.

Well, her 15 year old daughter loved it. She was already serving God. She said that it inspired her to "totally sell out".

Is Heaven Big Enough for Both of Us?

"When is the sequel coming out?" She asked me.

If she only knew how much she had inspired me to keep on writing. I'll tell her someday that "Part Two was for you."

Then this woman let her 17 year old daughter read it. She woke up in the middle of the night and gave her life back to Jesus.

And finally, her 19 year old, who was stripping at a local club read it. A couple of days later she came to church to meet me. We had a great visit. She is so incredibly beautiful, and so delightful.

I get angry when I think that society could allow her to be taken advantage of for their own pleasure. Mostly men, but women, too.

Why do they think that they have the right to use young girls to fill themselves up with? That is no way to treat a queen. And she is a queen. I am so glad that she is in the palm of God's hand and wherever she goes, Jesus will be with her.

"Okay. Who else do you want me to give it to, Jesus?" I asked.

"That's better. Those two ladies, and her." I glanced over to see who He was talking about.

"Her?" She was a successful business woman who had her life together and was serving God. I did notice a pained look behind her forced smile.

As I approached her, I asked her to come to my car. I was about to break my word to the church and give her my book.

"I have something for you." I said, as I explained that I wasn't even sure that I should be giving her the book, but I felt that I just had to. As I handed it to her she gasped.

"I was just asking Jesus how I could get a copy of your book. This is wild." She was so thrilled that she hugged me and then ran to tell her husband. I saw her that night and she looked different.

"Gina, I thoroughly enjoyed every page or your book. Thank you so much for writing it." She went on to tell me of her past experiences in witchcraft and the occult. She had been living with guilt and pain. As she smiled about the guilt being gone, I noticed that the pained look behind her smile was gone. She looked happy.

"Jesus, you were right. I mean, really right. I even feel like it was worth every bit of the pain that I have gone through in my life to see these women set free. Thank you so much for showing me that you do turn all things around to work for the good. You can make anything a blessing. You can even use damaged goods."

"Did you know that they can turn a sow's ear into a silk purse?"

G.L. Johnson

Jesus asked me, giggling. "Now, give a copy to those two ladies."

"Okay. But I have got to get permission first." I replied.

I felt that I needed to ask the church first. By trying to submit to their demands, I found that I was not obeying Jesus.

By obeying Jesus, I was in rebellion with the church.

Over a year had past so I hoped for the best, as I went to talk with the associate pastor. His wife had seen the good, so maybe he had seen it too. I could only hope as I approached him.

He said that when something just keeps coming back to you, it's usually God. He said that he had read my book and thought that it was anointed. He saw the good. He told me to obey God.

So I gave the ladies a copy. They were so excited after reading it, that they wanted to put it on the Internet.

"The world needs this." Was their response.

Suddenly I knew how the Apostle Paul felt as I was called into the office again. Is it better to obey God or man?

"I thought that we told you not to share that book at this church. And you agreed." They began. I was really glad that I had gotten permission, so I began with my defense.

"I agreed. But, I felt led to share it so I got permission."

"You are a liar and you are in rebellion." They accused.

I was stunned. Why couldn't they see that it was God? What was so wrong about me? I was only trying to obey God.

"These are my sheep." The pastor steamed.

"I don't want your sheep. God told me to write a book, not . ."

"God didn't tell you to write that book. God doesn't talk to people like you." He said, scowling at me, and breaking my heart.

I stood there shocked as the church that I loved so much and had given so much to, told me to go away and not to come back.

Then his wife interrupted him, telling me that I could stay, if I would repent and admit that I was lying. She said that if I would promise "not to tell" anyone, then I would be welcomed to stay.

Only, I didn't feel very welcome. I was crushed. I loved these people, but I couldn't stay where I was being tolerated instead of celebrated. I couldn't stay where I was not needed or liked just the way I was created to be. Me. Not a clone. Me.

So, as I lie awake wondering what my next move should be, I knew that my steps were directed by God Himself, and what ever came my way, God was in charge, and not me, and not them.

"Don't tell? Don't tell?" These were the two words that had come with every beating, every rape, and every evil.

"Don't tell . . . God should I tell?" I wondered.

But, I had other concerns. We were now living in a tiny two bedroom dive. I mean a real dump. It was on the third floor of a really disgusting building. It was so very little that there were no closets. The bathroom was so small that there was no room for a tub. But, at least we had a shower.

And, we had terrible credit, so there was no way that we could get a loan. Even if we got a loan, I'd probably blow it.

"Jesus, I know that without you I will never have a house. I need help. I need you to give us a house."

"Gina, I taught you my ways. Just like farming, when you want something, you have to plant seed." He gently reminded me how to do things His way, which was totally different than my way.

"If you want tomatoes, you plant tomato seed. When you want an apple tree, you plant an apple seed. If you want a house, then plant a house seed." He said.

"Okay, Jesus. I'll plant a house seed. To who? Where?"

"That lady, right there. Pay her house payment this month."

"But that's the wife of, he thought that my book was darkness. And she thought that it was even worse than darkness." I cried.

"Yes, but that is where I want you to plant your house seed." Jesus was very specific as to where he wanted us to plant our seed.

Planting it somewhere else would be a waste of seed and I could not afford to waste any seed at this point.

"Give me strength, Jesus. You want me to give my money to someone who thinks that I'm evil? Someone who looks down at me? What are you thinking?" I protested. But we wanted a house and we knew that Jesus knew what He was doing.

"So, a house payment is maybe $500 and that is not too bad."

Bobby and I talked it over and agreed. So I approached her.

"How much is your house payment? We would like to pay it for you this month." I almost fell down when she answered.

"1,000 dollars." She said, surprised at my offering.

"Oh, I thought that God said $500." I whispered, gulping.

"Oh, I was believing for $500." She answered, gratefully.

I felt good about the $500 until I got into our car.

G.L. Johnson

"God told me to ask you if you are believing Him for half of a house?" Bobby said as I closed the car door.

If I hadn't been sitting, I probably would have fallen down.

I told Bobby about the conversation that I'd had with this woman.

"I am sorry Jesus. Please forgive me for being stingy with your money. I can trust you to give me this house seed, right?" I asked.

We gave them $1,111, which included an extra 10% to cover the tithe, which is the part that you are supposed to give to God after you receive a blessing. We were so excited to give them the money, that I simply forgot that they had a low opinion of me.

She and her husband hesitated but accepted our seed.

"I'm sorry that it is so much." They said.

"Don't be sorry." I laughed through the pain. "My house is only costing me one thousand dollars." They had no idea of the sacrifice we were making, believing that we had heard from God.

So as I lay there, I wondered if God does talk to people like me? "Do you talk to people like me, Jesus? Do you?" I prayed.

That is when I got the news that the Nevada Supreme Court had rejected Patrick's appeal upholding the death penalty. A new date of execution would be ordered. He was still alive, on death row. 21 years had passed since the first time I had heard his name. 21 years had gone by since Jesus had asked me to tell Patrick that He loves him. 21 years, Jesus had kept him alive, waiting for me to tell him.

Chapter Fourteen
His Kingdom

"Seek first the Kingdom of God and His righteousness, and all these things will be given to you.
Matthew 6:33

"You know, Jesus, I would seek 'Your Kingdom' if I knew how to. Tell me, is 'Your Kingdom' a place? Show me what You mean. Show me what You want." I heard His answer over and over in my head,

"Seek first My Kingdom, if you seek after My Kingdom, I will give you everything that you desire."

As I stepped into our small, little shower, I said to Jesus,

"Well, if You want me to seek 'Your Kingdom', I guess You'll just have to show me how." I began to sing. I love to sing in the shower. Soon, I found myself inside of a vision.

I was flying over the city. It was a gloomy, rainy, day. I was seeing it in faded black and white. You could feel depression all around. It felt like there was a feeling of gloom and of despair. Then, I noticed that the buildings, houses, cars, fences, furniture, and all kinds of "stuff" had big red "For Sale" signs on them. The signs put off a greedy, jealous, pride-filled spirit. This was a very unhappy place and I didn't like being there. I flew on.

As I turned the corner I came up to a huge translucent gate. It looked almost like a thin sheet of water glimmered across the entry. Over the gate read "The Kingdom Of God."

I flew through to the other side and entered into a whole new dimension. The air was light and the colors bright. It smelt fresh, like flowers. There was such a peaceful easy feeling that felt great. As I flew closer to the ground, I knew that this was a place where all people were happy. This was a place were all were accepted.

There were still houses, cars, buildings, furniture and all kinds of "stuff" all around, but this time all the signs were blue and they read "FORGIVE". I could hear laughing and rejoicing. Off of the signs came a spirit of love and joy. I wanted to stay.

G.L. Johnson

And then, I was suddenly, back in the shower. I dried off and dressed quickly, heading for the living room where Bobby was watching TBN. I was happy to see him.

"Hey, honey, what are you doing?" Bobby asked.

"I was just taking a shower." I wanted to tell him about the "trip" but wasn't quite sure what to say. "Whatcha watching?"

"Creflo." I sat down to watch. He was talking about, you guessed it, The Kingdom of God. He said that anytime you read "Kingdom of God" in the bible, replace it with the words "God's way of doing things."

"God's ways. That's it. Seek first God's way of doing things and all things will be given to you. God, that's what I have been doing all along. I am seeking Your ways. Does that mean that You are going to give me the desires of my heart?"

I had been afraid to even desire anything. Afraid that it would be taken away. I was sure to make a mistake, and blow it. Afraid that my dreams would never come true, I dared not even dream.

"Gina, listen closely. If you don't dream, then it can't come true. You have to allow yourself to dream. I promise you, Gina, I will perform the thing that is appointed for you, I have to."

When Jesus said that, I ran and got my English translation. I opened it to Job 23:14.

I had recently been at a job that was 85% Russian. They were awesome people. While I was there I got to share Jesus with them. Most of them were Jewish, but a few believed in Jesus. They helped me to translate when necessary. Being from Russia they were afraid to talk about their faith openly. But I was glad to acquaint them with freedom of speech and freedom of religion in America. They got liberated.

Anyway, I bought all of my Jewish friends each their own bible written in Russian. Their reactions varied. Some came running for one, while others pleaded. But one special memory lingers. When I tried to hand my friend, Misha his copy, he said,

"I can't take that. I'm Jewish."

My reply was simple,

"It's okay, Jesus was Jewish."

"Oh, okay." He said. And took it. He was excited to read something in his own language.

Another time, the owner's father-in-law came to me and asked me if he could have one. He wanted it because it was his heritage.

Is Heaven Big Enough for Both of Us?

"This is not only my heritage it is my language." He even asked me to sign it and told me he would never forget me. What beautiful people.

"Jesus, was it such a big deal for them to have Russian bibles?" He answered me simply by giving me a bible that was in American English. Something that I could understand in my native language. The answer was

"Yes."

There is such a difference in being able to understand and grasp what was meant when you read it in the language you understand. So I got out my English bible and read.

"He will fulfill what He has planned for me; that plan in just one of the many that He has." Job 14:23.

If He has planned it then how could I doubt it? So with our house seed in the ground, we waited. Then came the test. We had given our rent money as part of our house seed, but I wanted a house, and as crazy as it may seem, I trusted God. So we went camping.

The first month was pretty nice. The camp grounds had agreed to open early for us, so we were the only guests. It was very peaceful.

The second month started out by raining for the first two weeks.

The kids, all three, and I stayed inside for two weeks of non-stop rain. I stepped on more crayons and hot wheels than I could count, or cared to count. I thought of how Noah's wife must have felt, when finally, it stopped raining. And then the sun came out. With the sun, came the heat. But, our Ark had air conditioning. It was so hot that we all stayed inside for two more weeks. I had had enough.

As I tried to find peace, Satan laughed.

"You're not camping. You're homeless. You are such a fool to believe that God would give you a house if you 'plant house seed'. He mocked. Then I heard my mother's voice.

"You'll never own a house. Not without an education. You'll never have enough money. You'll have to sell your soul for a house. But don't worry, there's always public housing." She said.

I had to hold on. The only way I knew to hold on was to cling to God's Word, and to His promises. When Jesus was tempted by Satan in the wilderness, he used the Word of God as his defense.

Three times Satan tempted Jesus and three times Jesus replied that,

"It is written." And that was my only defense.

If I couldn't trust God to keep His word by now, then I had better stop and look back at my life. I needed to read my own book again.

So, I started at the beginning and soon, I remembered all the times that Jesus had been there for me. Even though I had done it to myself, and had gotten myself into all kinds of messes, Jesus was always my way out, never letting me down.

So I held on to His promises. After all, God himself had told me to plant the house seed. I can trust Him, can't I?

His word says,

"Seek first God's way. <u>Give</u> and it will be given to you, pressed down, shaken together, and over flowing, men will give to you. God said that if you tithe that He would open the windows of heaven to you, and pour out a blessing, that there would not be room enough to receive it all."

Yet, behind all the promises of God, I heard my pastor's voice haunting me . . .

"God doesn't talk to people like you. God does not talk to people like you." He had scowled at me.

So I asked God again, as I started the portable electric stove to cook Bobby's dinner.

"Do you talk to people like me, Jesus? Do you? Or am I a fool to believe?" I waited for an answer.

Bobby jumped out of the car as he got home from work. He wasn't as full of camping as I was, so I wasn't surprised to see him in a good mood. It seemed as though he was always in a good mood, lately. He trusted Jesus and it was starting to show.

I could tell he had something pretty exciting to tell me but I didn't want to hear it. That is, unless he was planning to tell me that God had given us a house. If not, he could just go gather firewood and tell the trees his good news.

"Gina, guess what?" He flirted with his information.

"What?" I managed to grunt.

"God have us a house." He rejoiced.

"What?" I said much clearer. "Tell me exactly what you mean." This was not a joking matter.

The Lord has put some wonderful people in our lives. His word says that whatever you are willing to give up for the sake of the gospel, He would give you 100 times that back. He is faithful.

"They bought some land to put cattle on and the house is just sitting there empty. They said if you want it, you can have it."

We moved in July 1, 1999. We had planted our house seed mid April, 1999. Add it up. 2 ½ months later we moved into our new home.

It sits on 187 acres, so there's plenty room for a garden. I have learned a lot about farming and sowing seed. You see Jesus compared His Kingdom, His ways, to farming ways. God is teaching me His ways in a whole new way.

When we were planting the garden, there was a proper time to plant. The package told you when and where. It was important that we sowed at the right time and in the right place.

When God tells you to do something, or to plant a seed, don't wait two weeks or two months. Get out there and plant.

When we planted, we expected a harvest, but like God said, there was not room enough to receive it all. So what we don't have room for, we give away. If there isn't room for something, then, I believe that it belongs to someone else. Some blessing come to you, while others go through you.

God said that He would make you rich so that you can be generous in every occasion. Give, give, and then give some more.

He has moved us into a place that there is so much room. The view is great and the neighbors can't even hear my singing, they're so far away. It is a dream come true. One of many dreams.

"It needs some fixing up, but I like it out here." I told Jesus.

"Stay here for now, but this is not your house. I will lead you to yet another place, but for now, stay here." Jesus said. "And, do remember, what you are willing to walk away from, for my sake, will determine what I will bring to you. In My Father's house are many mansions, and I have prepared a place specifically for you. So, enjoy yourselves, and, I will prepare you for your future. I will tell you when and where to go from here." He instructed.

Doing things God's way works. That's the way to go.

"God, that was so easy. I'd like to do something else 'Your Way'. What else can I do?"

"Pray for those who persecute and use you."

"Pray for who? Are you serious?"

Chapter Fifteen
His Purpose

"I will praise You, because I am fearfully and wonderfully made."
Psalm 139:14

"Fearfully. What could that mean? Were you afraid to make me? Afraid that I would not live up to your standards? Afraid that you wouldn't be able to find a purpose for me?"

"Gina, you are confused about purpose. I did not create you and then give you a purpose. I had something very specific in mind when I planned you. You have heard that I completed the work before I ever began it?"

You see, before God begins to make something, He determines a need. He decides what it is that He needs or wants done, and what exactly He needs to create to get that job done, or fulfill that need. Then He takes everything that would be necessary to fulfill that need and puts it inside of the creation. Or the "creature".

Take the microphone. Man had a need to transmit sound to an amplifier, so that the amplifier could amplify sound. Determining the need first, he then made a blueprint, putting everything inside the microphone that it would take to transmit the sound to the amplifier. Inside, is everything necessary to fulfill its purpose.

The same with you. God has a need that only He knows of. So He created exactly who He needed to fulfill that need. Then, He placed you exactly where you would learn what you needed to learn in order to fulfill that need.

God is God of all. Not just the saved. God is God of all creation. The saved have just chosen to serve Him already. When the time comes for you to fulfill the need that you were created for, God will have your attention, too. YOU CAN RUN BUT YOU CAN'T HIDE.

Let me add that inside of the microphone is NOT everything that is needed to pump gas. It was not created to pump gas.

The gas pump was created to pump gas, not to transmit sound to the amplifier. I cannot do your job for you, nor can you do my job for me. We need each other. Only you can be you.

G.L. Johnson

"Now, Gina, about this living up to my standards. I made you distinctly different for the same purpose that I created you. Now, do you think that you can just be yourself?"

"Yes, but is that enough?" I asked.

"Yes, I need you to be yourself. If you won't be yourself then you become useless to me." He said.

Look at Pharaoh. Do you think that he chose to be the one to tell God, "No." Do you think that he wanted to be who he was. By saying "no" he brought many plagues onto his people. But, God was in control of him as well as you. By the end of it all, Pharaoh asked for God's blessing.

"Go and be gone, Moses, and ask your God to bless me also."
Exodus 12

And King Darius, he had Daniel thrown into the Lions den, and made lots of mistakes. He said to Daniel, *"Your God is God."*

And what about Adam? Let's look at him. Everyone gives Adam such a hard way to go. He did exactly what God created him to do. You see, He was created to prove our need for Jesus.

When Adam fell, he started in motion God's plan that Jesus had finished. Keep in mind that He finished everything before He began to lay the foundations of the earth. Adam had to fall. And it had to be Adam, too, because in him was the seed of all mankind. So in his falling, he was a success.

"I put in him everything that it would take for him to fulfill his purpose, including his desire for fruit." Then God asked me,

"Why do you question my reasons for doing things the way that I choose?" That was a good question. What gave me the right to question what God does or His motives?

"I'm sorry, God. Sorry for trying to think for you. You are God and not me. Please forgive me, again?"

"Gina, you don't have the right to question anyone's motives. That is my job, not yours. Work on the beam in your own eye."

He was right, so I repented.

"The heart of a king is in My hand, and I will turn it as I choose." Jesus said, reminding me that He was not an after thought to fix man's mistake. No, He was our Savior before the foundations of the earth were laid, by Him. He is our creator. I've heard such things as,

"If man had never fallen, there would have been no need for Jesus. We would have simply been face to face with God."

Who exactly do they think walked with Adam in the cool of the garden? Jesus himself said,

"I Am the first and the last. Before Abraham was, I Am."

Jesus was not created. He created. No need for the Creator? What were they thinking?

*"All things were made by Him: and without Him was not anything made that was made. In Him was life, and that life was the light of men . . . He was in the world, and the world was made by Him, and the world knew Him not. But as many as received Him, to them He gave power to become the sons of God, even to them that believe **on His Name**." John 1:3-4, 10*

After looking up the words Abba and Patter in Hebrew and Greek, I discovered that the original word for father meant: The Source, the one that sustains.

Then I decided to look up the original Hebrew word for son, as used in the scripture, *You are the Christ, the son of the Living God.* And the original word for son means: The Inward, Inside essence of God, thrust out of. The actual inside essence of God thrust out.

Jesus is the insides of God thrust out into this world. Jesus is the Source Himself becoming flesh.

Then Jesus told me a little story about the chief firefighter.

"He was the boss. He was in charge. He trained all of his crew to be the best. They were all qualified firefighters. They were all heroes.

The chief lived in a nice house with his wife and children. He loved them very much and supplied all their needs. He gave them everything that was his. He was their father, their source.

One day while working he got a call that his own house was on fire and his family was trapped inside. His own children were going to burn.

Having the authority to send any of his crew inside to save his family he chose to go inside himself. Risking the pain of fire and death, he went in himself to save them from destruction."

"Gina, don't you think that I love you enough to come myself?"

"Yes, Jesus, I know that you came yourself. I saw you."

"You know, Gina, just because Adam fell and Pharaoh said, "no", that does not give you the go ahead to fall or say, "no" to me. You were not created to be Adam or Pharaoh. You were created to be Gina. Did you know that Gina means Queen?"

"Yes, you already told me that." I blushed.

"Just reminding you. There is another thing that I want to discuss with you, Gina." I knew that I was about to learn something quite important. So I listened. "You must not believe this lie." He said.

"What lie? Or should I say, which lie?"

"I did not create man out of dirt, but, I created the body of man out of the dust. I created the house out of dirt. Are you made of brick because you live in a brick house?" He asked me.

That made so much sense.

"I, God, spoke to myself. I breathed my breath into man and he became a living soul. Stop the lie, now. When I said that 'You are gods, and sons of the Most High' did you think that I was lying? Can I lie? Your body is the temple or house of the living God."

We are God material. Made out of the same things as God. The same spirit that raised Jesus from the dead lives inside of us.

Do you think it would be strange for your child to say to you,

"I'm a human. I am a man child."?

It doesn't concern you if they act like humans either, but if they start to bark like a dog... now you're concerned. It is when they sin that you are concerned, right?

You are God's child. So why do you think that it is so strange to say, "I am a child of God. God's child. A Godchild."

God expects you to be like Him. It's when you start acting like the devil that concerns Him. It is not natural for you to sin. You are going against your nature. That is why it bugs you so bad to do wrong. Unless you are hardened by your past pains or drunk, it probably bothers you when you sin. Quit going against your nature and act like your Source.

"Do you know, Gina, that you are fearfully and wonderfully made."

"I better look that up before I say anything." I responded.

Fearfully: To make with great care, afraid of making a mistake.

Wonderfully: In a manner to excite wonder or surprise. The original sense is Awe. A miracle. President Johnson was quoted as saying, "We cease to wonder at what we understand."

Now, that was different. Not at all what I expected.

"So, Jesus, You already needed me before you created me, fearfully and wonderfully? That is just so hard to believe."

"I don't make mistakes." He assured me.

"But, I've always heard that You don't need me. That You will just get someone else to do what I won't do. Is that true? Or, do you need me, Jesus?" I asked anxiously.

"Gina, <u>no one can do what I created you to do the way that you would do what I created you to do.</u> Do you understand that your purpose is more important than what happened to you?"

"My purpose? More important? Are you saying that the church was wrong about me? Are you saying that I have a purpose? Well then, please tell me, what is my purpose?" I waited for His answer.

I wanted so much to hear that I had a purpose, yet still I could hardly believe my ears. I have a purpose, but I'm damaged goods. What could God have possibly created me to do. What could my purpose be?

He answered my question with more questions. His plan was to make me realize my own purpose, by looking inside of myself, and so, He asked,

"What is the first thing that you think of in the morning?"

"The first thing I think of in the morning?" I asked Him back.

"What is the thing that you love doing so much that it consumes you?" He asked, making me really think about my answers.

"What do I love doing so much that it consumes me?" I asked back.

"What do you dream of doing instead of a job? What would you do whether you got paid to do it or not? What is it that just keeps coming back, from inside of you, even when it's been squished, squashed, and pushed aside? Think about it, Gina, you know what your purpose is." Jesus said. "Think about it."

The same for you. Think about it. When you get up in the morning, if all you can think about is singing, then you are supposed to be a singer. Or, if all you can think about is preaching, then you are supposed to be a preacher. If all you can think of is defending people, then you are supposed to be a lawyer. And, if when you get up, all you can think about is writing, then you are supposed to be a writer.

I thought about it, and Jesus was right. I do know my purpose. The real question is,

"Do I really trust Jesus enough to be myself?"

Chapter Sixteen
The Call

*"What I tell you in the dark, you must repeat in broad daylight.
And what you have heard in private,
you must announce from the housetops."*
Matthew 10:27

"You know, Jesus, a lot of people think that I don't hear from You. They think that I'm a nut, a real flake. At times, I'm tempted to side with them. What do You think?" I asked Him.

Softly, I heard his reply.

"Gina, do you remember 20 years ago, when you prayed this, 'Jesus, give me the answers. When I speak, let the words come from you. When people look at me, let them see you. And, help me to serve you in the middle of it all.' You asked me for that. Do you remember asking me for that?" Jesus asked me.

"Yes, Jesus, I do. But that was so long ago." I reminded Him.

"I put that desire in you. I want the same. Don't let go of your desire to serve me. Keep your eyes on me, not man. You are exactly who I created you to be, and I am well pleased." He said.

"But I have done some pretty stupid things in the last 20 years. I've offended and caused ~~some~~ many to stumble. Are you sure that you are 'well' pleased?" I asked, cautiously.

"Gina, you haven't done anything that I can't fix. You have made mistakes. But that only proves that you have tried. Besides, a mistake is merely an opportunity to learn the correct way, and as long as you seek after my ways, I will be well pleased with you. Now, since we are talking about mistakes." Jesus said.

"Who brought up mistakes?" I thought.

"You did." Jesus answered.

"I'm listening." I said.

"What gospel are you preaching?" He asked.

"What do you mean, 'what gospel?' I'm preaching the gospel of Jesus. Is there any other?" Dumb question.

"That is just what I mean. Why? Shouldn't you preach the gospel that I preached?" he asked, simply.

"What? Your death, burial, and resurrection? Is that what you preached?" I asked.

"I never preached that. I shared that only with my closest friends." Jesus answered, patiently.

"You must be born again. That was what you preached?" I was sure that I was right.

"Actually, I never preached that either." He corrected me.

"What are you saying? You did to preach that." I argued.

There I was, arguing with my maker again.

"No, I didn't. I mentioned it once to an old man who came to me in the middle of the night. 'You must be born again' was the response to his question. He wanted to know how he too could enter into the 'kingdom' that I spoke of."

"Wait, Jesus, did you say kingdom?" Suddenly, I got it.

"Exactly. Look in Mark 1:14, after being tempted in the wilderness and after being ministered to by angels,

I came to Galilee preaching the gospel or good news of the 'kingdom of God', saying, 'the time is fulfilled and the kingdom is at hand: repent and believe the good news.' The Kingdom is here. Repent."

When He said that, I ran to look up the word repent.

Re: to do again or come again. Pent: on top. We get penthouse from the same root word. So, come again to the top. Change your way of thinking back to your original top position way. Or you could say,

"Get back on top. God's way is here."

Jesus had brought me all the way back around to "The Kingdom". Seek first His ways. I was finally getting it.

"It's Your ways that You want to teach me. Your ways."

Then I noticed in the bible that everywhere that Jesus went, he talked about the Kingdom. The Kingdom of God is like . . .Life inside My way of doing things is like a treasure that a man finds.

Then He showed me something that I will not forget.

"Why do you think that the church is having such a hard time influencing the world?" He asked me.

"The church is like . . ." He began. "The church is like a man who owned a jewelry store. He had the finest of jewels, the most precious of stones. Everything that you could want in a jewel or stone, his store carried. The man decided to make a commercial to advertise his store.

Is Heaven Big Enough for Both of Us?

The entire commercial focused on the front door. Never once did the commercial mention the precious stones or the wonderful jewels. They just went on and on about the door. They told you all about the door but neglected to show where the door led. You need to tell them about the jewels of My kingdom. And that is what My church is not doing. They tell you all that they think that they know about me, and never bother to tell you what's inside. What exactly is the treasure of doing things My way? It's in hooking up to My ways that will bring 'new life'."

"But shouldn't we show them that You are the only door?"

"Gina, if a person really wants what is inside the story, he will find the door. I am easy to find. What is important is what happens to you once you get inside of doing things My way. Tell them what the Kingdom has in store for them." Jesus said.

That is what being born again is all about. You are born into God's kingdom. You start to live and think like a citizen of a kingdom that is built on love. In God's kingdom you must do things the way the king has instructed in order to remain in the kingdom. So if you do things the way that God wants, you will be a citizen of His kingdom. Get it?

Then I asked him, just to clarify one more thing,

Do you want us to seek You or Your Kingdom? Don't You want us to seek Your face, and not what is in Your hands?"

"I said to seek <u>first</u> My kingdom and all things in my hand will be given to them. First means first. First seek My ways and My face will be there." He continued, "And why do people try so hard to get into My presence? Don't they know that they are always in My presence? I am everywhere." He explained.

We need to understand that about our God. God is everywhere, He sees everything. He makes the sun shine on the evil and the good. We need to quit struggling to get into His presence. We are already there. Now act like it.

This is what King David wrote about his and your ever present Lord in Psalm 139.

"Lord, You have examined me and You know me. You know everything I do; from far away You understand all my thoughts. You see me whether I am working or resting. You know all my actions. Even before I speak, You already know what I will say. <u>YOU ARE ALL AROUND ME ON EVERY SIDE.</u>

"You protect me with your power. Your knowledge of me is too deep, it is beyond my understanding.

G.L. Johnson

"Where could I go to escape from You? WHERE COULD I GO TO GET AWAY FROM YOUR PRESENCE? If I went up to heaven, You would be there. If I lay down in the world of the dead, You would be there. If I flew away beyond the east, or lived in the farthest place in the west, YOU WOULD BE THERE to lead me. You would be there to help me.

I COULD ASK THE DARKNESS TO HIDE ME or the light around me to turn into night, but EVEN DARKNESS IS NOT DARK FOR YOU, and the night is as bright as the day. Darkness and light are the same to You.

"You created every part of me, You put me together in my mother's womb. I praise You because I am fearfully and wonderfully made. I KNOW IT WITH ALL MY HEART.

"When my bones were being formed, carefully put together in my mother's womb, when I was growing there in secret, YOU KNEW THAT I WAS THERE. YOU SAW ME BEFORE I WAS BORN.

"The days that have been allotted to me had all been recorded in Your book, before any of them ever began.

"O God, how difficult I find Your thoughts, how many of them there are. If I counted them, they would be more that the grains of sand. WHEN I AWAKE, I AM STILL WITH YOU.

"Examine me, O God, and know my mind. Test me, and discover my thoughts. Find out if there is any evil in me and GUIDE ME IN YOUR EVERLASTING WAY" Psalm 139

Now, how hard do you think it is to get into the presence of someone that is already in your presence?

Think of it this way: if you are in the same room with your children, how hard would it be for them to get in your presence.

They are already there. And if they wanted your attention, they would just call your name. The same with you and God. You are already there. So don't try so hard. Just bask in His presence.

Enjoy His presence but don't forget to talk to Him. You can sit in someone's presence and never say a word. But don't do that.

Jesus called you his friend because he wants to be your friend. Friends talk. Friends tell each other their secrets. They have a secret place that only they can go together.

The more time that friends spend together in their secret place the more they know each other. When you come out of that secret place with God you will know His will and His ways.

And then you can go . . .

"And, as you go, preach, saying, 'The Kingdom of Heaven is at hand.' Heal the sick, cleanse the lepers, raise the dead, and cast out devils: freely you have received, freely give." Matthew 10:17

Then, I remembered the blue FORGIVE signs.

Chapter Seventeen
Church

*"The group of believers was one in mind and in heart.
None of them said that any of their belongings were their own,
but they all shared with one another everything that they had."*
Acts 4:32

As I lie awake wondering what my next move would be, I asked Jesus.

"Why? Why did You send me to that church in the first place? You knew what they believed, and that they would judge me as inadequate. Why did You want me to go there?" I asked Jesus.

"Gina, let me ask you something? What did you learn while you were being judged and rejected?"

"So very much. I learned a lot of what not to do and how not to treat people. How not to treat people like you are better than them. How not to turn people away. How to let people give what they have to give, what ever is it. I did learn a lot about faith and authority and covenant rights. Okay, I withdraw my question."

"It is amazing who I can use to teach you something. I was also giving those who rejected you a chance to be rewarded." He said.

"Rewarded?" For what?" I asked.

"Whoever welcomes you, welcomes me. You can be sure that whoever gives even a drink of cold water to one of the least of my followers, because he is my follower, will certainly receive a reward." Jesus said.

"Yeah, I read that before in Matthew 10:40."

"Let me tell you who I meant when I said the least of my followers. I was not merely talking about the ones with the least, or the ones who came from the least, or the ones that look like the least. No, I was talking about the ones <u>that you like the least</u>."

"Oops, I did it again. I am sorry but I missed the meaning of that one, too. I must bless the people that I like the least? Is that what you are telling me. Jesus?" I asked.

G.L. Johnson

"Yes, Gina, you must bless the least, for my sake." He answered. "And, I would like to show you more of my ways."

"Please show me, Jesus. I really want to know." Or did I really want to know . . .

As I sat, looking around our "new church", I wondered what it was that was missing. It was so noticeable that I couldn't ignore it.

"What is it?" I wondered.

"It appears to be pride." Jesus said.

"What?" I asked.

"Pride. That is what appears to be missing. It sure feels different, doesn't it? Just remember, things aren't always as they appear." He said.

I sat there quietly repenting. I didn't want any part of pride. The more I thought about it the more determined I became. I didn't have anything to be proud of except Jesus' mercy and His grace. And I had not earned that.

He gave me His mercy and grace because of His character. That is what He is made of. Nothing that I can do can make Him love me any more than He already does. I can not earn His unconditional love. Going to church does not make me any better than those who don't go to church. It is not church that makes you a child of God. You are a child of God because God's your daddy.

"Gina, get past the mistakes. Not only your mistakes but everyone else's mistakes. Put all that away and just love. Simply love." Jesus instructed me.

"Love? All right. And, please help me to stay focused on Your ways. Help me to serve You. I know that if I serve the ones that You want me to serve, then I am serving you.

"If you serve anyone, you are serving me." He added.

"Like a waiter, I focus on taking Your order and serving it to You, promptly, with a smile on my face.

I do believe that the size of the tip depends on three things.

1. Did you get what you ordered? 2. Did you get it when you wanted it? 3. Did you get it served happily? What? When? And How? What do you think of that?" I asked.

Jesus agreed that good service deserves a good tip.

"Your tips are good, too. I love serving you." I added.

"Good. Then give that lady right there a copy of your book."

"Oh, no. I'm going to talk to the pastor, first." I stammered.

I gave it to my new pastor and He read it before giving me his opinion. That was a good sign.

"This should be a movie." He joked.

He was so down to earth. So cool as he admitted,

"I would hate to see you have to explain to God why you only shared 100 copies instead of 100,000." He explained.

So I gave her a copy and she thanked me as she explained how her father had terribly mistreated her and abused her.

"He hated me and blamed me for even being born." She explained. She is so beautiful, too, and talented, but full of pain.

"Since I read your book, I am able to look at life differently." She said, thanking me for writing it. She is one of the most tender hearted people that I know. After all the pain and suffering, to be even a little gentle would be next to impossible.

"Gina, I want you to tell my people that being clothed in humility, does not mean humiliation. I do not humiliate them in order to humble them." Jesus said.

Boy if that wasn't the truth, what was?

"Please continue, Jesus?" I urged Him.

"My way is to show you my ultimate love. My goodness humbles you, not humiliation." He continued. "Tell them that it is not being humble to say 'I'm worthless, You paid too high a price for me.' I did not pay a price that was too high." He said. "I paid the price that it took to cover the cost." He explained. "They are not worthless. Even before they were born, they were worth my life. I paid the right price. They were worth my life from the very beginning." He assured me.

Then Jesus showed me that **real pride** is saying that you are anything less than what God said that you are. How dare you exalt your beliefs above God. Believing that you are a looser above what God said about you. That is true pride. That is what Satan did when he said that he would exalt himself; his beliefs, his kingdom, his ways above God's throne.

But to be humble to God is to say: I am who God said that I am. I can do what God said that I can do. I have what God said I have. That is being submitted to God and His word. And so, I repented.

"Gina, I can't even begin to tell you how much your book has blessed me." My new friend, Paul, told me. "But I do want you to know that all eleven people that I have shared your book with have gotten saved. Thank you so much for writing it." He told me.

He is now in the process of writing his testimony. I can't wait.

"Hurry up, I don't want to be late." Bobby said as he rushed out the door to start the car.

There was a special speaker at church and Bobby was running the video production, so we hurried out the door.

In our rush to get to church, we treated each other ugly. As we bickered, our tones got uglier. Joshua spoke up.

"Mom, you know, when to talk to someone like that, you are actually talking to Jesus." He said, teaching us all a new way.

"Let me out of the car." Bobby said, not wanting a 5 year old boy to be the one to teach him this great revelation.

And it was. I finally got it. The way I treat you is how I am treating Jesus. Talk about a new level of respect. I would never treat people the same again. And, by the time we got to church that night, we were all different, thanks to a 5 year old boy.

The speaker was great, too. He broke down scripture and brought it down to earth. He taught us that we all were created with a built in receiver so that we could hear from God.

Jesus made each of us with our own receiver, so that He can communicate with each of us directly.

We got two great messages in one night.

As I handed the guest speaker a copy of my book, he joked,

"I could just wait for the movie to come out?" he said laughing.

I practically fell over. Now there's a prophet.

Debbie grabbed me on the way out of church,

"Hey, Gina, we need to talk? Here's my number. Call me in the morning, tomorrow, please? I really need to talk to you about something important." She said.

We had just met within the last couple weeks, so I had no idea what it could have been about. I told Bobby,

"It sounded important. Maybe she wants us to pray with her for somebody, or anoint someone's house or something."

I called her early the next morning.

"Gina, are you believing God for anything?" She asked me.

I could have gone on and on with a list of things, but at the time, I drew a blank. I had to sit down as she continued. "Let me put it this way, I feel like God wants me to give you my truck."

She was giving me exactly what I had asked God for. A Chevy Blazer. Only it was in Mint Condition. I had never expected one so nice.

It is beautiful. Both inside and out. Far more than I could have ever done for myself. God is so awesome.

Just two weeks ago, as we drove to church, the kids were in the back seat, wining about how there just wasn't enough room. They were going on and on. I was fed up, so I turned around and said,

"Why are you crying that there is not enough room? Just ask God for a truck if you want more room." Then as I turned around,

"And make it a Chevy Blazer, either black or white will do."

God and Debbie gave me a gray Chevy Blazer two weeks later.

Now we drive down the road in total awe of God, still amazed.

"This is what You want for us? Something this nice?" I finally understood what He meant by 'His Goodness humbles you.'

"Gina, your thinking that you are not worthy of my best is pride. You are worthy. Do you remember your seed?" he asked.

Then I remembered the van. Someone had given it to us. It was absolutely not what I was hoping for. When I saw it for the first time I smiled at the couple saying, "Thanks!" and I thought to myself,

"Please God not this?" I hoped.

"Nice seed." Was God's reply.

"But who would want it?" Was my next thought. Then God explained that if I rejected their seed, I would be cutting off their blessing. I had been hurt before, when my gifts were looked down at, so I knew that my attitude was in desperate need of work.

"This is exactly what I have been believing for." Was Sara's response when we pulled into her driveway.

I was glad she wanted it and she was glad that I didn't. That was over two years ago. I had gotten so wrapped up with my book that I had forgotten about the seed.

And then Jesus said something that I will never forget.

"Have you ever had something to give, but no one to give it to? Have you ever had a story to tell, but no one to tell it to? A song to sing, but no one would let you sing it?"

"Yes, Jesus, You know that I have." I confessed.

"Gina, being blessed is so much more than what people do for you. It is what they allow you to do for them." Jesus explained.

"What they allow me to do for them?" I asked.

"Yes, Gina, think about it. Do you think that a famous songwriter is happy because he's rich and famous? Or is he fulfilled because people

G.L. Johnson

are listening to what he has to say. They are listening to the message that came from inside of him?"

The writer is blessed because he is able to give of himself fully to others, from the inside out. And the people let him give.

I had so much to give and needed to give it.

"Thank you, Jesus, for bringing us here. I have been so blessed. Thank you for leading my steps. And thank you for what has happened to bring me here. Bless all my friends that I had to leave behind and give them joy and peace."

"Are you forgetting someone?" Jesus asked.

"Yes, please bless my enemies. Show them Your mercy. Make them as happy as You have made me?"

Chapter Eighteen
Our Healer

*"And these signs will follow them that believe:
IN MY NAME: will they cast out devils;
they will speak with new tongues; they will take up serpents;
if they drink any deadly thing, it will not harm them;
they will lay hands on the sick, and they will recover."*
Mark 16:17-18

As I poured myself some Kool-aide, I asked Jesus to heal my headache. My head was pounding and I was in need of his touch.

"Heal your own headache." He replied.

"That is rather rude, Jesus. After all, You are the healer. Why do you mock me? I need a touch from You, Jesus." I said as I washed down two pills with the Kool-aide. It was awful. I had forgotten the sugar. I grabbed the sugar, pouring it into the pitcher. Just then, Joshua came in.

"I wanna be the taste tester, I wanna be the taste tester." He sang.

I gave him a taste.

"Perfect." He praised gesturing for more. Sierra joined us.

"I want some from the pitcher." She asked, with a slight whine.

"It's the exact same thing, Sissy." Josh enlightened her holding out his glass to her.

"Okay." She took a drink of his and off they ran, laughing.

"What Joshua just said about the glass is true." Jesus said. "Think of me as the pitcher and yourself as the glass. The exact same stuff that is inside of Me is inside of you. I am your Source. You came out of Me. Which means simply, you can heal your own headache. Do you understand?" He asked.

"I think so." I answered.

When your body is sick or injured, it is normal for it to get better. You were created to heal naturally. Your body should always try to heal itself. It is natural for it to be healthy and whole.

"You have inside of you, Me. My essence. Think of it like I am the ocean. If you take a bucket of water out of the ocean and bring it to Ohio, you have all of the essence of the ocean in the bucket. You don't have the whole ocean in the bucket, but you do have the essence of the ocean in the bucket. You are a bucket of me in Ohio. I created you in My image. And that is why when someone wants to taste Me, they should be able to taste me, through you." He explained.

"Wow. You are saying that I have the power to heal. I'm a godchild. I'm not so sure about this." I hesitated. "Please, help me to understand what You really mean, here. Don't let me get lopsided here. I can see a thin line between right and wrong."

"Gina, try not to throw out the good teachings with the bad. You have the power to do everything that I did and more. My word tells you this:

'He that believes in Me, and the works that I do, he will do. And greater works than these will he do. John 14:12

But there is a very important thing that you must not leaves out. You must stay vitally connected to Me. My word says:

'Abide in Me, and I in you, as the branch can not bear fruit of itself, except it abide in the vine; no more can you, except you abide in Me . . . for without Me, you can do nothing.' John 15:4

"Do you know what abide means?" He asked me.

"Yes, I do. It means to live in. Like you abide in your home."

"I have told you this so that My joy may be in you and that your joy may be complete. My command is this: "Love one another just as I love you. The greatest love you can have for your friends is to give your life for them. You are My friend if you do what I command you to do." He continued. His voice was so warm, I listened, hanging on to every word that He spoke.

"I do not call you a servant any longer, Gina. Because servants do not know what their master is doing. Instead, I call you friend, because I have told you everything I heard from My Source." Then what He said blew my mind. "You did not choose Me, I chose you and appointed you to go and bear much fruit. The kind of fruit that endures."

"Wait, just a second. I thought that I chose to serve You?" I tried to make that sound like a statement, but it was a question. I was stumped at the thought that I did not have a choice. Before the foundations of the world were laid, Jesus Himself had chosen me. Now that was unbelievable. Who would have thought? I knew that would take a while to sink in. But, He was reading straight out of the bible, and He was reading it straight to me.

"Wake up, the coffee is brewing." I thought to myself.

Is Heaven Big Enough for Both of Us?

"That's right. I said, *'you did not choose Me, I chose you and appointed you . . .and so The Source will give you whatever you ask of Him in My name. And this is what I command you: Love one another."*
John 15:16

I sat there thinking about the people in my life.

"Love one another, the same way that I have loved you. When you were the one hurting others, I loved you. And that wasn't all that long ago." He reminded me. "And, look at how My love has changed you. Your love has power because it is My love inside of you. Please, love one another. People's lives depends on whether or not you follow this rule."

Just then Summer Breeze came over to me and put her finger on a scratch that I had on my arm.

"Don't touch." I said as I pulled back my arm.

She looked at me as if I was totally missing the point.

"What are you doing, Mom? I have the healing power of Jesus in my hands." She declared.

"I'm sorry." Reaching my arm out, I added, "Please, heal me."

"Get in line with what Jesus says and be healed." She said.

Kissing me, she ran out of the room. She believed what she said. And that was that.

"God, give me that simple childlike faith. You said it and I believe it. Period."

I sat there remembering the Doctor's words,

"If you do not close the hole in her heart, she will not live to be older than one." He had said.

Well, ten years later, Summer Breeze still has that hole in her heart, only now the doctors say that it was caused by a rare genetic disorder called William's Syndrome which has now caused severe pulmonary stenosis. That means that the arteries going into her lungs are extremely narrowed, so narrowed that there should be such severe pressure, that her heart would explode. Only, in her case there is a hole in her heart that is relieving the pressure. A hole that shouldn't be there, but it was there before we knew why. Therefore, the very thing that was supposed to kill her has saved her life.

"She is a miracle." The doctor said, holding his hands up to heaven. "I wouldn't touch her, she is a walking miracle."

We are so glad that we listened to Jesus ten years ago, when he had asked simply,

"Gina, do you trust me?"

"Yes, Jesus. I trust you." I had answered.

"Then trust me." He had said.

As I stood there thinking, trying to understand, I tried to see things through the eyes of Jesus.

The very thing that was supposed to kill her, has saved her life. The very thing that was supposed to kill her, has saved her life.

"The very thing, just like Patrick, the one that was supposed to kill me, saved my life. Talk to me Jesus." I asked him for some understanding. "Help me understand this thing, Jesus."

"I created Patrick. I needed him, so, I created him. I put into him what he needed in him to be able to fulfill his purpose. I want him to know that I love him and I will not let go of him. I want him to know that I am inside of him, too." Jesus said. "Help him to see passed the anger and the pain, into himself, where I am." Jesus said. "Patrick has been chosen and created for my great purpose, and he will help to lead many people to trust in Me. He is my son, my creation, tell him that I am well pleased." Jesus said.

"Wow. So be it, Jesus." I responded.

That night I found out that the Nevada Senate had voted on Friday April 16, 2001 to tentatively endorse a death penalty moratorium in Nevada. This would be a two-year memorandum while a major study into capital punishment is conducted. The Las Vegas Sun reported.

Senate Judiciary Chairman Mark James, Republican, from Las Vegas succeeded in getting a voice vote favoring his plan.

"This amendment is not against the death penalty," James said, "but the best possible analysis is needed because a death sentence is a grave and difficult and irreversible decision."

James said a moratorium is needed until a comprehensive study can explore issues such as socio-economic and racial bias in capital cases, effectiveness of the death penalty as a deterrent, DNA testing and the cost of carrying out a death penalty compared with no-parole life sentences.

James got support from Senator Bob Coffin, Democrat from Las Vegas, who said that 38 years ago he was nearly beaten to death by a 17 year old, Patrick McKenna, who is now on Nevada's death row for murder.

"I have held vengeance in my heart for all these years" Bob remarked, "but the bible says, and I believe, that vengeance belongs

Is Heaven Big Enough for Both of Us?

to the Lord." Bob voted in favor of the moratorium. I lowered the newspaper in awe.

Jesus had made it possible for Patrick to live at least 2 more years. Would I have time to tell him thank you?

Then Jesus repeated himself, and said, reminding me,

"That's right." He said, "you did not choose Me, I chose you and appointed you . . .and so The Father will give you whatever you ask of Him, in My name. And this is what I command you: Love one another."

John 15:16

Chapter Nineteen
The Answer

*"I came into the world for this one purpose,
To speak about the truth.
Whoever belongs to the truth listens to me."*
John 18:37

Doesn't it sound so simple. Love one another. But is it? Could I lay down my life for a friend? What about an enemy? Or even my pastor? I don't think so.

"Jesus, I think that you chose the wrong person. I can't do it."

"Gina, I did not create you and then give you a purpose. Now, think about it, would I ask you to do something without giving you the ability to do it?" Jesus asked.

"No that wouldn't be cool. I know with you all things are possible, but does it have to be so unbelievable?"

"If you can believe the unbelievable, then you can move mountains with your voice. Just by speaking the word. Do you believe that the same power that raised Me up from the grave, lives inside of you? I mean, do you really believe it?"

He waited for my answer. Cautiously, I answered Him.

"Yes, I believe." I said with assurance.

"Now stop believing it and know it." He said.

"What are You trying to teach me, Jesus?" I asked.

"Okay, follow me here. Do you know that Egypt is in Africa?"

"Yes, I know that." I responded confidently.

"You don't know that. Have you ever been there? No. You believe what you see on the map. You believe what you have been told." He clarified the difference between knowing and believing.

"Once that you have 'been there', then you know that it is there." He continued, "You believe with all your heart that Egypt is there, but you can only know for sure if you have been there."

"Yes, You are right, I believe the map, I believe the bible, too."

G.L. Johnson

"Do you believe in Me or do you know Me? Have you 'been there?' Have you experienced Me, felt Me, seen Me? Am I in you or do you just believe that I am?" He questioned me.

"Wow. Well, I used to just believe, but now, I know that you are real. I know that You are God. I know. You are right. I know because I have been there." I admitted.

"Good. You do know. Did you also know that My word says that *'as a man thinks, so is he.'* It does not say as a man believes." He clarified.

"Did you know that you can believe what I am saying all day long, but until you know that it is the truth, it is only what you believe. Understand?"

"Yes, Jesus, and I know that what You are saying is true. I know it is." I had to admit it, He made me see things clearer.

And, I do know for certain that Jesus is real. I saw Him.

"Good, since you know, now, I tell you: love your enemies. Bless them that curse you, do good to them that hate you, and pray for them that spitefully use you and persecute you. So that you may be the children of your Source. For he makes the sun to rise on the evil and the good and gives rain to the just and the unjust.

"Why should I reward you if you love only the people who love you? And if you speak only to your friends, have you done anything out of the ordinary? Even the unsaved do that." Matt 5:44

"Jesus, I know that you have given me the ability to do just that or You would not ask me to do it. I know that if I love you, I will do what you ask. I know that I can do anything as long as I am vitally united to You."

"Is there something else?" He asked.

"Yes, there is. Thank You for my enemies. Because of them, I have the opportunity to please You by doing things Your way instead of mine."

"Gina, I want to show you something that My word says,

'Do not deceive yourselves, no one makes a fool of God. You will reap exactly what you plant.' Galatians 6:7.

"Do you believe this?" He asked me.

"No. I don't believe it, I know it." I said confidently.

"Good. I wasn't just talking about things, but of actions, thoughts, and feelings. Do you follow what I'm saying?"

"Yes. You mean like give mercy, get mercy. Give forgiveness, get forgiveness. Give love, get love. Give help, get help."

"Exactly. By the way, Gina, do you know what exactly means? Why don't you go ahead and look it up?" Jesus suggested.

Exact: accurate in every detail with something taken as a model. Perfectly complete and clear in every detail.

"Then give, knowing that you will get back exactly what you have given out. If you pray heartfelt prayers for your enemies, then you will receive the same. *'if a man's ways please Me, I will make even his enemies to be at peace with him.' Proverbs 16:17*

What could I say. I had been there, too. I knew that what Jesus said was truth. I had to do things His way. After all, that is what being in His Kingdom is all about.

I had wanted so much to know what He meant when He said, "Seek first My Kingdom", that I couldn't ignore what I had just been taught. It is my responsibility to act on what I know.

Stupid is when you don't have the knowledge. But when you ignore the knowledge that you have, that makes you ignorant. I was not about to ignore what Jesus was saying.

"Gina, I promise to not give you more than you can handle, but I do have one more thing to show you. Do you really want to know about My ways?" He asked me.

"Yes. Please show me." I answered.

"Get out your bible and follow Matthew 5:22.. I'll read.

"Now, I tell you: if you are angry with your brother you will be brought to trial, if you call your brother 'you good for nothing' you will be brought before the council." I breathed deep as He continued.

"If you call your brother a worthless fool you will be in danger of going through the fire of hell."

"Oh my. I am so sorry. Lord, I can't even remember how many times that I have done that. Oh, Lord, please forgive me."

"So, if you are about to offer your gift to God at the alter and there you remember that your brother has something against you, leave your gift there in front of the alter. Go at once and make peace with your brother, and then come back and offer your gift to God. Blessed are the peacemakers for they will be called the children of God. Now go and sin no more." He finished.

"If You are pleased with me," I prayed, "teach me <u>Your ways</u> so that I may know You, then I will continue to find favor with You." *Exodus 33:13.*

G.L. Johnson

"I will give you the keys to <u>doing things My Way</u>. What you prohibit on earth will be prohibited in heaven. What you permit on earth will be permitted in heaven." Matthew 16:19

"Blessed is he, whose greatest desire is to do what God requires; **God will satisfy them fully**. *Blessed are those who are persecuted because they do what God requires;* **<u>My Way of doing things</u> belongs to them**.*" Matthew 5:6*

"God, I want to know you more, to go deeper. Teach me how to pray."

"Gina, have you not heard that I am the same yesterday, today, and always. I'll show you again, but it is the same. Pray like this:

*"Our Source in heaven, **Holy is Your Name**.*
Your Kingdom has come
Your will must be done *on earth as it is in heaven.*
You give us *each day our daily bread.*
You forgive our debts *as we forgive our debtors.*
You lead us not into temptation*.*
You deliver us from Evil*.*
To You belongs the Kingdom,
The Power, and The Glory, Forever." Matthew 6:9-13

"My Ways are so simple, please don't make them deep."

"I'm sorry." I said again.

If I could only trust God instead of trying to do things my way.

"Jesus, I surrender. Change what you need to change and fix what you need to fix. I'm Yours."

I can only tell you how important it is to do things God's Way, **but understanding the value of it can only come from Jesus.**

As I arrived at choir practice, Jesus reminded me of a dream I had. You see, my heart ached to sing. I wanted to sing with everything that was in me. But no one would let me sing. Mom said that I couldn't and Dad asked if I wouldn't.

"Please don't sing. It hurts my ears." He'd say.

So I buried my dream.

"Jesus, please let me sing to you." I begged.

"Gina, understand this. In the beginning, Satan was the anointed angel of praise. He led the band. When he fell, he gave up his microphone to man. When you sing, it burns him. You are doing what he was created to do before he became twisted. That is why he does whatever he can to try to stop you from singing. I love your voice. And I love the way that I made it. Sing for me."

At 39, there I stood, between two awesome singers. and to put icing on the cake, Jesus made it possible for us to sing on the TBN Praise The Lord program. When the pastor asked us to pray about the taping, I said,

"I've been praying about this for 20 years."

He laughed, but I was serious.

During the taping, I noticed that some people were treating a black woman rather rudely. I was stunned when I heard the words of prejudice and hatred toward her. We were in church. Did they not realize that the very spirit of Jesus lives inside of her. I felt so bad. There was nothing I could say so I simply gave her a hug and said, "I love you."

I began watching a little closer, and noticed just how bad we regard and mistreat people who are a little different than ourselves right here in America. I was guilty of doing the same.

"Jesus, I am so sorry if I have ever judged or treated anyone as less than what I would treat you." I prayed. "I realize that You live inside of each person, whether I like it or not. I am sorry for ever judging anyone. And I know that I have done it many times over. Please forgive me."

"To any one that I have mistreated or looked down at, I am truly sorry. I apologize. I honor and look up to you. I pray that you will have peace and feel welcome to be yourself. We all need you to be yourself."

"Gina, I live inside of you, too." Jesus said. "Can you just be yourself?"

"I'll try." I promised.

Chapter Twenty
Your Hope Of Glory

*"God's plan is to make known His secret to His people.
This rich and glorious secret which He has for all peoples.
And the secret is that Christ is in you,
which means that you will share in the Glory of God."*
Colossians 1:27

"I will share in the glory of God? Wow. What is this glory that I get to share in?" I asked.

"Well, look it up and see." Jesus urged me.

Glory: Distinguished praise or honor; exalted reputation; Adoration and praise offered in worship; A wonderful asset. The height of one's triumph, achievement, or prosperity. To rejoice with jubilation.

"**THE HEIGHT OF ONE'S TRIUMPH?**" I asked in wonder.

"That is right, Gina. Because My Spirit lives and is alive inside of you, because you have Christ inside of you, and you are vitally united to me, you do have **TRIUMPH IN SPITE OF IT ALL.**"

God is so big that He is able to love each and everyone of us the "most." We are all His "favorite."

The Word says that God is not a respector of persons. No, He respects faith. So if He has done anything for anyone, then He will do it for you, too, if you are willing.

"My friends, what good is it for one of you to say that you have faith if your actions do not prove it? Can your faith save you?"

"Suppose there are brothers and sisters who need clothes and don't have enough to eat. What good is there in you saying 'God bless you. Stay warm and eat well!' If you don't give them the necessities of life? So it is with faith: if it is alone and includes no actions, then it is dead. But someone will say, "One person has faith another action. Show me how anyone can have faith without actions? I will show you my faith by my actions." Is my answer to that.

You believe that there is only One God? Good. The demons also believe and tremble with fear. . . As the body without the spirit is dead, also faith without actions is dead. James 2:26

G.L. Johnson

"Hey, Gina, remember Larry?" Jesus asked.

"Yeah. I wonder how he's doing."

"He's in the palm of My hand." Jesus assured me.

About a year and a half ago, my girlfriend Sara called me. She had just finished reading my book and wanted to know if Bobby and I had time to come over. We did.

When we arrived she asked us if we would anoint her house for her. She said that she felt something evil going on. Her husband, Larry was out of town. We started in the attic and worked down.

Bobby called us to come down to the basement. Sara looked shocked as we stood there in front of an altar. There were goblets and daggers and all the stuff that is used for performing Satanic Rituals.

"I guess I need your permission to destroy it?" Bobby said.

"Go for it." Sara agreed. Bobby tore down the altar as I prayed. After he was done anointing the basement and claiming it back for the Lord, we prayed in agreement over Larry's picture, that he would turn and serve Jesus. We took all the occult objects and threw them inside of a dumpster.

"That was great." Bobby said, smiling.

About 2 months later, Larry joined us at church. Bobby and I, both were amazed when he walked to a much different altar and gave his life to Jesus. He renounced Satan, publicly. Awesome.

"Gina, would you go west for me?" Jesus asked.

"Talk to Bobby about it and I'll start packing." I answered.

The hard part would be telling Lisa. My baby sister. We had become such close friends over the years that just the thought of moving more than 20 minuets away was too much.

"How can you just walk away from the house and everything? And what about my babies. Don't you want to be around them?"

"Yes, Lisa, I love your babies. But we feel that we have to go west. We have to do something there. I don't even know where it is we are supposed to be going, but we have to go." I told her.

"Are you crazy, Gina?" Lisa asked.

I know I must have sounded insane, but I could not ignore Jesus when He asked me to do something. I knew that with Him it is always an adventure, so we started giving away most of, and selling some of, but for some reason, I held on to a lot of our stuff.

"California, here we come." We sang with excitement.

The kids were thrilled. They wanted to go to Disney Land, but little did I know, we were on our way to the Los Angeles Zoo.

"I just can't believe this place." I told Bobby. "It's really changed. And the prices. How can people live here?"

I'm not sure what we expected, but it wasn't this. There were hundreds of families living on the streets. I'm talking about families with no dads, families with no moms, families with both parents but no jobs, families with teenage children, families with little babies, all of them, families with no place to call home.

They were forced to live on the streets and in the parks, some fortunate enough to sleep overnight in a shelter for the homeless.

It was so sad to see so much wealth all around and right there mixed through it, so many children without homes and beds and meals. I cried for the state of California, and it's children.

We went to the beach. What a beautiful place to get away from the reality of what was happening to society. After a day in the sun we stopped at a local store for an ice cream cone and I got a job.

That is where I met Jerry. He was my boss. He was a lot of fun to work with, and we closed down the store at night, so there was lots of slow time when we would talk. Jerry was a really cool guy, and we got along great.

Jerry was an atheist and he refused to talk about God. As far as he was concerned, there was no God.

Since it's not my job to convince him, or persuade him, I didn't bother. Instead, I told him about the night that I had been kidnapped by a killer. He was captivated. He wanted to know all about that terrible night and the man that did the crime.

He went home after work and looked up Patrick McKenna on the Internet, and found out that everything I had told him was true.

He came to work the next day with a print out on Patrick and he was full of questions. He wanted to know all about it.

"I wrote a book about it, if you want to read it." I told him.

"Yeah, I do." He replied. This kind of stuff excited him.

I gave him a copy of my book and waited.

"Wow. Great book. There was a bit much Jesus for me, but I read the whole thing. I think that you should publish it." He said.

That night as we shared miracle experiences, Jerry started to admit that maybe, just maybe, there was a God. He said that he wasn't ready to call on Him yet, but if he ever found himself in a situation where he needed to, he now knew who to call on for help.

Later that week as we were closing the store, we joked.

"If Conrad doesn't come to work tomorrow, then I'll believe that God is real." Jerry laughed as he challenged God to a duel.

"You're on. So, if he does show up . . ." We laughed.

As I drove to work, I looked forward to a day of work without Conrad. I walked into the store and Conrad was standing there.

"Jerry." I called over to him.

"What?" He said, looking over.

"You were right. There is no God." I admitted.

"No. No. You can't give up yet. I just started to believe." He answered, adding, "God is real." That was good enough for me.

Within weeks, my work changed to an office position at a mortgage company, where I would get enough overtime to afford our $1400 a month motel room. The months that had five weeks were $1750.

We did get clean towels everyday, and our room did come with a kitchenette. It was perfect for a single person, but we had five.

Bobby's checks gave us plenty of money to blow trying to stay away from "home". But, we got even closer in the next few months than we thought possible. We got along great and enjoyed our time together on our sight seeing trips of California.

It was especially nice visiting Vicky. God had somehow healed the wounds and brought us back together.

As we sat around the Thanksgiving Day meal that Vicky and Bobby had prepared together, we gave thanks for family, friends, and forgiveness. Yes, Vicky had forgiven me and it was so nice.

Vicky had left the music business and was now running her own international marketing firm. She had quite the mind for business. She was also successful at love and was in the process of planning her wedding. I was glad to see her so happy.

For Christmas, Vicky took us to Disney Land, making Summer Breeze's dreams come true. Summer got to meet her favorite people, or should I say mice. I was especially fond of Minnie Mouse's house.

A few months, and thirty books later, our mission ended and Jesus told me that we could return to Ohio.

"Well done." He said. "Thanks."

We were packed and on the road within days.

Sure, there was lots of beauty in California, but the heartless, homeless, carelessness turned the beauty gray. It made the beauty fade away. California left me feeling sad for her.

"Lisa, we're coming home." I said.

"Thank God." She said.

As we arrived in Ohio, I thought back to a cold spring day in 1978, and as we crossed the Ohio state line, I cried.

Somehow, I felt like I was home, and there is no place like home, even if it is cold and icy. I know, home is where the heart is, and as long as we have each other, where ever God leads us, that will be home, but somehow, I felt like I was home.

"We insist." Lisa and Joey said. "You can stay here as long as you need to." They were so happy that we were home.

Lisa called to Lilliana, as we drove into the parking lot.

"Look, Lill, Aunt Gina is home. Aunt Gina is home."

It sure was nice to be home, even though we still needed to find a home, it was nice to be home.

Within the week we moved into a beautiful townhouse with a huge yard. We got the kids into school and got comfy in our new home.

They were so happy to be back in Ohio. It was perfect, so I sat down to write, adding another chapter to my book, and as I finished writing, I remembered hearing the voice of Jesus.

"Tell my children to stop trying so hard to make it happen, and let it happen. Relax, and let it be. Tell my people to breathe. I will do the rest. With every breath, they'll breathe in more of me and more of my power."

I believe that He is talking to you who have called on Him. If you have, then all you have to do is trust Him and breathe. You probably can't dream as big as what God has in store for you. And if you do dream that big, then what are you waiting for? Let God bless your dreams. Jesus will make all of your dreams come true.

Wherever you go, He is already there, just waiting to bless you, waiting for you to let Him bless you. So, let Him bless your life.

"The Lord God breathed His life-giving breath into the man's nostrils and the man began to live." *Genesis 2:7*

I believe that you will begin to live when you breathe in the life-giving breath of Jesus. So, breathe Him in.

The most important thing for you, is to realize that the very God that created the universe has chosen to live inside of you.

G.L. Johnson

So, how will you let Him live inside of you? Will you let Him love and breathe His peace through you, or will you grieve His Holy Spirit with the things that you do and say?

Jesus not only lives in you, He lives in the person that is standing next to you. If you can learn to treat others the way that you would treat Almighty God, then, love could prevail.

"So, Jesus, you just want them to breathe?" I asked.

"Yes, breathe." Jesus said.

"Breathe and obey." I added.

Jesus laughed. "Just tell them 'Breathe.'"

"Okay." I said. There were many things that I wanted to add. But Jesus simply said,

"Breathe. And give that lady over there a copy of your book." Then He added, "And don't wait forever."

"Okay." I gave her one the next time I saw her.

"Gina, thank you so much for your book. It's perfect. God has really blessed me through it. I am going to give it to my best friend. She is an Emmy Award Winning Producer. I think that your book should be a movie, Gina."

She was so excited, and I was so shocked.

As I drove home, I joked with my best friend, Jesus.

"Well then how about Kate Winslet, or Julia Roberts, or Sandra Bullock with red hair? And for Bobby, there's Brad Pitt, or Keanu Reeves, or even that new guy, what's his name?

"Gina, do you trust me?" Jesus asked.

"Yes, Jesus, You know that I do." I answered.

"Then, just breathe, Gina, and I'll do the rest." He said.

As of August 6, 2004
Patrick McKenna awaits execution at Ely State Prison.

He is now confined to a solitary cell for 23 hours of the day.
He is transferred to a small, cement enclosed cell to exercise for one hour every day and he is allowed to shower every third day.

Patrick says that he prefers this kind of a life rather than death.

For over 24 years Patrick has lived on death row . . .
Waiting . . .

About the Author

Inspired to make a difference, G. L. Johnson reaches inside herself to expose the root of evil. Determined to not let a painful and abusive childhood stop her from living a joy filled life, she searches to understand the forces behind the sickness of her abusers, one on death row this very day.

Freedom rings as she takes a stand to love her enemies. Reaching to find triumph in spite of it all, she has learned to live and love through forgiveness.

Hoping to inspire other's to reach past their pain and into the future, where their dreams are waiting, she is living proof that there is a future after failure.

Printed in the United States
25567LVS00005B/157-159